Meet Tyler Jacobs and Nell Regan in the third book
of Diana Palmer's exciting trilogy LONG, TALL
TEXANS!

"You can't learn to swim if you keep balking at the water,"

Tyler said, lifting her chin. "You're going to have to
come out of your shell, little one, and start looking
around you."

"I don't understand." Nell shifted restlessly, but he
wouldn't let go of her.

"Very simply, Nell, if you want me, you're going to
have to believe in yourself a little and start trusting
me not to hurt you."

"Trust comes hard," Nell said, although what he
was saying was more tempting than he realized. She
did want him, terribly, but she was playing for keeps.
Was he?

"It comes hard to most people." He smoothed the
hair away from her face. "It depends on whether or
not you think it's worth the chance. Love doesn't
have a money-back guarantee. There comes a time
when you just have to trust your instincts...."

Dear Reader:

The spirit of the Silhouette Romance Homecoming Celebration lives on as each month we bring you six books by continuing stars!

And there are some wonderful stories in the stars for you. During the coming months, we're publishing romances by many of your favorite authors, including Brittany Young, Lucy Gordon and Rita Rainville. In addition, we have some very special treats planned for the fall and winter of 1988.

In October, watch for *Tyler*—Book III of Diana Palmer's exciting trilogy, Long, Tall Texans. Diana's handsome Tyler is sure to lasso your heart—forever!

Also in October is Annette Broadrick's *Come Be My Love*—the exciting sequel to *That's What Friends Are For*. Remember Greg Duncan, the mysterious bridegroom? Well, sparks fly when he meets his match—Brandi Martin!

And Sal Giordiano, the handsome detective featured in *Sherlock's Home* by Sharon De Vita, is returning in November with his own story—*Italian Knights*.

There's plenty more for you to discover in the Silhouette Romance line during the fall and winter. So as the weather turns colder, enjoy the warmth of love while you are reading Silhouette Romances. Your response to these authors and other authors of Silhouette Romances has served as a touchstone for us, and we're pleased to bring you more books with Silhouette's distinctive medley of charm, wit and—above all—*romance*.

I hope you enjoy this book and the many stories to come. Come home to Silhouette Romance—for always!

Sincerely,

Tara Hughes
Senior Editor
Silhouette Books

DIANA PALMER

Tyler

Published by Silhouette Books New York

America's Publisher of Contemporary Romance

SILHOUETTE BOOKS
300 E. 42nd St., New York, N.Y. 10017

ISBN: 0-373-08604-0

First Silhouette Books printing October 1988

Books by Diana Palmer

Silhouette Romance

Darling Enemy #254
Roomful of Roses #301
Heart of Ice #314
Passion Flower #328
Soldier of Fortune #340
After the Music #406
Champagne Girl #436
Unlikely Lover #472
Woman Hater #532
Calhoun #580
Justin #592
Tyler #604

*Long, Tall Texans Trilogy

Silhouette Desire

The Cowboy and the Lady #12
September Morning #26
Friends and Lovers #50

Fire and Ice #80
Snow Kisses #102
Diamond Girl #110
The Rawhide Man #157
Lady Love #175
Cattleman's Choice #193
The Tender Stranger #230
Love by Proxy #252
Eye of the Tiger #271
Loveplay #289
Rawhide and Lace #306
Rage of Passion #325
Fit for a King #349
Betrayed by Love #391
Enamored #420

Silhouette Special Edition

Heather's Song #33
The Australian #239

DIANA PALMER

is a prolific romance writer who got her start as a newspaper reporter. Accustomed to the daily deadlines of a journalist, she has no problem with writer's block. In fact, she averages a book every two months. Mother of a young son, Diana met and married her husband within one week: "It was just like something from one of my books."

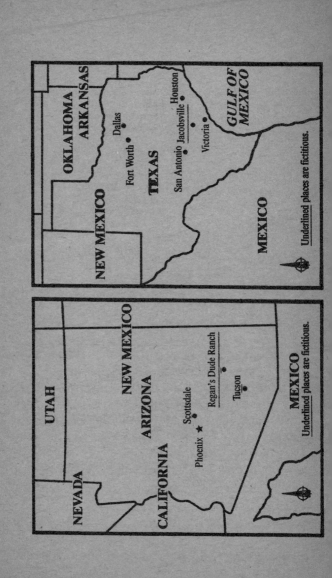

Chapter One

To Tyler Jacobs, the hot arid southeastern Arizona landscape still seemed about as welcoming as Mars, even after six weeks of working on the Double R dude ranch near Tombstone.

He was restless and vaguely depressed. He'd taken a day off to fly to Jacobsville for his sister, Shelby's, wedding to Justin Ballenger, a man she'd refused to marry years ago. Tyler was still puzzled by the courtship. They hadn't looked the picture of a happy couple, and he knew that Justin had been bitter toward Shelby for breaking their earlier engagement.

But it wasn't any of his business; he had to keep that in mind. And better to see Shelby married to Justin, who was old-fashioned enough to keep his marriage vows, than to see her mixed up with the local playboy attorney she worked for. Maybe things would work out for them. If the way Shelby had looked at Justin was any indication, they had to work out. She was obviously still deeply in love with him.

Abby and Calhoun had been at the wedding, too, and Tyler was relieved to find that his brief infatuation with Abby was over. He'd been ready to settle down and was unconsciously looking for the right kind of woman. Abby had fit the bill in every respect, but he wasn't nursing a broken heart. His eyes narrowed in thought. He wondered if he was capable of loving a woman. Sometimes he felt that he was impervious to anything more than surface interest. Of course, there was always the woman who could hit a man hard before he knew it. A woman like Nell Regan, with her unexpected vulnerabilities and compassion....

Even as the unwelcome thought touched his mind, his pale green eyes narrowed on a rider approaching from the direction of the ranch house.

He sighed, glaring through the endless creosote bushes. They dominated the landscape all the way to the Dragoon Mountains, one of Cochise's old strongholds back in the mid-1800s. The "monsoon season" had almost passed. Today it was on the verge of a hundred degrees, and damn what they said about the dry heat not being hot. Sweat was pouring down his dark olive complexion from the sweatband of his gray Stetson, soaking his Western-cut chambray shirt. He took his hat from his jet-black hair and drew his forearm over the wetness while he got his bearings. Out here one stretch of valley looked much like any other, and the mountain ranges went on forever. If elbowroom was what a man wanted, he could sure get it in Arizona.

He'd been out in the brush trying to round up some stray Hereford calves, while his worn leather chaps were treated to the double jeopardy of cholla and prickly pear cactus where the creosote wasn't so thick. Nothing grew around creosote. Having smelled the green bush, especially in the rain, he could understand why.

Before the rider got much closer, Tyler realized that it was Nell. And something was wrong, because she usually kept the length of the ranch between them. Their relationship had become strained unexpectedly, and that saddened him. It had seemed as though he and Nell would be friends at their first meeting, when she'd picked him up at the Tucson airport. But all too soon something had sent Nell running from him.

Perhaps that was for the best. He was earning a living, but not much more, and all his wealth was gone. He had nothing to offer a woman like Nell. All the same, he felt guilty if he'd hurt her, even inadvertently. She didn't talk about the past, and neither did anyone else. But Tyler knew that something had happened to make her wary and distrustful of men. She deliberately downplayed the few attractions she had, as if she was determined not to do anything that would catch a man's eye. Tyler had gotten close to her at first, because he'd thought of her as a cute little kid. She'd been so anxious to make him comfortable, sneaking him feather pillows and all kinds of little things from the house to make him feel at home. He'd flirted with her gently, teased her, delighted in her shy company. And then, like lightning, the housekeeper had made him see that the child he was playing with was really a twenty-four-year-old woman who was misinterpreting his teasing. From that night on, he and Nell had somehow become strangers. She avoided him, except at the obligatory square dance with guests twice a month.

Nell did seem to find him useful in one respect. She still hid behind him at those every-other-Saturday-night barn dances. The way she clung to him was the only crumb left of their easy first acquaintance. But it was vaguely insulting, too. She didn't consider him a threat in any sexual way, or she'd have run screaming from his presence. He'd made some hard remarks about Nell to his sister, Shelby, but he hadn't really meant them. He hadn't wanted anyone to realize how Nell was getting to him.

He sighed, watching her approach. Well, she wasn't dressed to fan a man's ardor, in those baggy jeans and blouse and slouch hat, and that was a good thing. He found her shyness and his odd sense of empathy for her disturbing enough without the added complication of an exquisite figure. He frowned, wondering what she looked like under that baggy camouflage. As if he'd ever find out, he thought, laughing bitterly. He'd already scared her off.

He wasn't a conceited man, but he was used to women. His money had always attracted the beautiful ones, and whatever he wanted, he got. And so, being snubbed by the stone girl stung his pride.

"Have you found those strays yet?" Nell asked with faint nervousness as she reined in beside him.

"I've only gone through five thousand miles," he murmured with soft antagonism. "Wherever they are, they're probably enjoying the luxury of enough water to drink. God knows, except in the monsoon season, they'd need a divining rod or second sight in this barren wasteland to find any."

Nell searched his hard face quietly. "You don't like Arizona, do you?"

"It's foreign." He turned his gaze toward the horizon, where jagged mountains seemed to change color as the sun shifted, first dark, then mauve, then orange. "This takes some getting used to, and I've only been out here a few weeks."

"I grew up here," she remarked. "I love it. It only looks barren. If you see it up close, there's all kinds of life."

"Horny toads, rattlesnakes, Gila monsters..." he agreed dryly.

"Red-winged blackbirds, cactus wrens, roadrunners, owls, deer," she corrected. "Not to mention wildflowers by the score. Even the cacti bloom," she added, and there was a sudden softness in her dark eyes, a warmth in her voice that was usually missing.

He bent his head to light a cigarette. "It looks like desert to me. How's your trail ride coming?"

"I left the guests with Chappy," she said with a sigh. "Mr. Howes looked as if one more bounce would put him on the ground. I hope he makes it back to the ranch."

Tyler smiled slightly as he glanced at her rigid figure in the saddle. "If he falls off, we'll need a crane to get him back on."

Nell grinned without meaning to. He wouldn't know it, but he was the first man in years who'd been able to make her smile. She was a somber, quiet woman most of the time, except when Tyler was around. Then she'd found out what he really thought of her...

"Tyler, could you take over the camp out for me?" she asked unexpectedly. "Marguerite and the boys are coming for the weekend, and I have to go into Tucson and get them."

"I can handle it, if you'll persuade Crowbait to cook," he agreed. "I'm not making biscuits again. I'll quit first."

"Crowbait isn't so bad," she defended. "He's—" her dark eyes narrowed as she searched for a word "—unique."

"He has the temperament of a cougar, the tongue of a cobra and the manners of a bull in heat," Tyler said shortly.

She nodded. "Exactly! He's unique."

He chuckled and took another draw from his cigarette. "Well, boss lady, I'd better get those strays before somebody with an itchy trigger finger has beef for supper. I won't be long."

"The boys want to go looking for Apache arrowheads while they're here," she added hesitantly. "I told them I'd ask you."

"Your nephews are nice kids," he said unexpectedly. "They need a firmer hand than they get, though."

"Marguerite isn't the ideal parent for two high-strung boys," Nell said defensively. "And since Ted died, it's been worse. My brother could handle them."

"Marguerite needs a husband." He smiled at the thought of Marguerite. She was like the life he'd been used to—sophisticated and uncomplicated and pretty. He liked her because she brought back sweet memories. She was, in fact, all the things Nell wasn't. "But a dish like Margie shouldn't have much trouble finding one."

Nell knew her sister-in-law was beautiful, but it hurt somewhere deep inside to hear Tyler acknowledge Margie's good looks. Nell was only too aware of her own limitations, of her round face and big eyes and high cheekbones. She nodded, though, and forced a smile to her unlipsticked mouth. She never wore makeup. She never did anything to draw attention to her...until recently. She'd tried to attract Tyler, but Bella's comments had killed the notion. Tyler's subsequent behavior had buried it.

Now Nell knew better than to make eyes at Tyler. Besides, Margie was just his style, she thought bitterly. And Margie was interested, too.

"I'll go into Tucson, then, if you're sure about the camp out. And if you can't find those strays by five, come back in and we'll let your Texas friends look for them in the morning," she added, referring to two of the older hands who shared a Texas background with Tyler and had become fast friends of his in the six weeks he'd been in residence.

"I'll find them," he said carelessly. "All I have to do is look for a puddle of water, and they'll be standing on their heads in it."

"You already know not to sit in any dips or washes," she murmured. "Out here is even worse than in Texas. It can be raining twenty miles away and the sky can be clear, and before you know it, you're in a floodplain."

"We have flash floods where I come from," he reminded her. "I know the dangers."

"I was just reminding you," she said, and hated the concern that she'd unwittingly betrayed.

His eyes narrowed and he smiled unpleasantly, stung by her condescending attitude. "When I need a nursemaid, honey, I'll advertise," he said in a pronounced Texas drawl.

Nell steeled herself not to react to what was blatantly an insult. "If you have a chance tomorrow, I'd like you to speak to Marlowe about his language. One of the guests complained that she was getting tired of hearing him swear every time he saddled a horse for her."

"Why can't you tell him?"

She swallowed. "You're the foreman. Isn't keeping the men in line your job?"

"If you say so, ma'am." He tipped his hat with faint insolence, and she wheeled her mount too quickly, almost unseating herself in the process when she pulled on the bit too hard. She urged the horse into a trot and soothed him, stroking his mane as she apologized. She knew Tyler had seen that betraying action, and she felt even worse. She was the last person on the ranch who'd ever hurt a horse voluntarily, but Tyler had a talent for stoking her temper.

He watched her go, his cigarette smoking, forgotten, in his lean, tanned fingers. Nell was a puzzle. She wasn't like any woman he'd ever known, and she had quirks that intrigued him. He was sorry they'd become antagonists. Even when she was pleasant, there was always the reserve, the bitter holding back. She seemed to become rigid when she had to talk to him.

He sighed. He didn't have time for daydreaming. He had to find six little red-and-white-coated calves before dark. He turned his horse and moved into the thick brush.

Nell dawdled on her way back to the adobe ranch house. She wasn't anxious to have Marguerite around, but she hadn't been able to find an excuse to keep the redhead away. Tyler's remark about her sister-in-law still rankled. He found Marguerite attractive, and it wasn't because of Nell that Marguerite was finding reasons to spend time on the dude ranch. She wanted Tyler. She'd made it obvious with her flirting.

Marguerite was beautiful, all right. She was redheaded, green eyed, and blessed with a figure that looked good in anything. She and Nell got along fairly well, as long as neither of them looked back nine years. It had been Marguerite who'd helped put the scars on Nell's young emotions. Nell had never been able to forget what had happened.

On the other hand, it wasn't until Tyler came that Nell really noticed how often Marguerite used her. She was impulsive and thought nothing of inviting her friends out to the ranch for horseback rides or of leaving her two young sons in Nell's care.

Those actions had never bothered Nell very much until lately. Recently, Nell had been feeling oddly restless and stubborn. She didn't like the idea of Marguerite coming for two weekends in the same month. She should have said so. Giving in to her sister-in-law had become a habit, the way of least resistance. But not anymore. She'd already given Marguerite some unmistakable signals that little Nell wasn't going to be walked over anymore.

Margie only came out to see the Texan, Nell was sure of it. She felt a sense of regret for what she might have felt for Tyler if he hadn't made his lack of interest so apparent. But that was just as well. Margie had made it obvious that she liked Tyler, and Nell knew she was no competition for the older woman. On the other hand, she was pretty tired of letting Margie use her for a doormat. It was time to say so.

Her sister-in-law and her nephews, Jess and Curt, were already packed and waiting when Nell parked the Ford Tempo at the steps of their apartment. The boys, red-headed and green eyed like their mother, made a beeline for her. At seven, Jess was the oldest. Curt was five and already a contender for a talking marathon.

"Hi, Aunt Nell, how about taking us to hunt lizards?" Curt asked as he clambered into the back seat a jump ahead of his taller brother.

"Never mind lizards, nerd," Jess muttered, "I want to look for arrowheads. Tyler said he'd show me where to look."

"I reminded him," Nell assured the older boy. "I'll go lizard hunting with Curt."

"Lizards make my skin crawl," Marguerite said. She wasn't quite as tall as Nell, but she was equally slender. She was wearing a green-and-white striped dress that looked as expensive as the diamond studs in her ears and the ruby ring on her right hand. She'd stopped wearing her wedding band recently—just since Tyler came to the ranch, in fact.

"Well, if I get a lizard, he can live with me," Curt told his mother belligerently.

Nell laughed, seeing her brother in the small boy's firm jaw and jutting chin. It made her a little sad, but it had been two years since Ted had died, and the worst of the grief had worn off. "Can he, now?"

"Not in my house," Marguerite said firmly. After her husband had died, Margie had taken her share of the ranch in cash and moved to the city. Margie had never really liked ranch life.

"Then he can live with Aunt Nell, so there."

"Stop talking back, you little terror." Marguerite yawned. "I do hope all the air conditioners are working this time, Nell. I hate the heat. And you'd better have Bella stock up on Perrier—there's no way I'm drinking water out of that well."

Nell got in under the wheel without any comment. Marguerite always sounded like a conquering army. It was annoying and sometimes frankly embarrassing to have Margie ordering her around and taking things for granted. Nell had taken it for a long time, out of loyalty to her late brother, and because the boys would suffer if she didn't. But it was hard going, and until just recently she'd taken a lot from Marguerite. It was only when Marguerite began making a dead set at Tyler that Nell had started talking back. And now that she'd gotten the hang of it, she rather liked not being talked down to and told what to do. She stared at her sister-in-law coldly while the boys argued in the back seat about who got the middle and who got a window seat.

"The ranch is mine," she reminded Marguerite quietly. "Uncle Ted is in charge until I turn twenty-five, but after that, I'm sole owner. Remember the terms of my father's will—my brother got half and I got half. Uncle Ted was executor. Then when my brother died, you got his share of the ranch in cash. As executor, Uncle Ted keeps control until I come of age. You don't give orders to me, and you don't get special consideration just because you're an in-law."

Marguerite stared. It wasn't like Nell to fight back so fiercely. "Nell, I didn't mean to sound like that," she began hesitantly.

"I haven't forgotten what happened nine years ago, even if you're trying to," Nell added quietly.

The older woman actually went bloodred. She looked away. "I'm sorry. I know you don't believe that, but I really am. I've had to live with it, too. Ted despised me for it, you know. Things were never the same between us after I had that party. I still miss him, very much," she added in a soft, conciliatory tone, with a glance in Nell's direction.

"Sure you do," Nell agreed as she started the car. "That's why you're dressed to the teeth and finding excuses to suffer the heat at the ranch. Because you miss Ted so much, and you want to console yourself with my hired help."

Marguerite gasped, but Nell ignored the sound. She pulled out into traffic and started telling the boys about the new calves, which kept the older woman quiet during the drive home.

As usual, when Bella saw Marguerite coming in the front door, the buxom housekeeper went out the back door on the pretense of carrying an apple pie over to the bunkhouse. On the way there she ran into Tyler, who looked tired and dusty and half out of humor.

"What are you doing out here?" he asked, grinning at the older woman with her black scowl.

"Hiding out," Bella said grumpily, pushing back strands of salt-and-pepper hair while her black eyes glittered. "She's back," she added icily.

"She?"

"Her Majesty. Lady Leisure." She shifted the pie. "Just what Nell needs, more people to take care of. That lazy redhead hasn't lifted a finger since poor Ted drowned in a dry wash. And if you knew what that flighty ex-model had done to Nell..." She flushed as she remembered who she was talking to. She cleared her throat. "I baked the men a pie."

"You baked me a pie," Nell muttered, glaring at her housekeeper as she came out of the back door. "And now you're giving it away because my sister-in-law is here. The boys like pie, too, you know. And Margie won't spoil her figure with sweets, anyway."

"She'll spoil my day," Bella shot back. "Wanting this, wanting that, make the bed, bring her a towel, cook her an omelet ... She can't be bothered to pick up a shoe or carry a cup of coffee, no, not her. She's too good to work."

"Don't air the dirty linen out here," Nell said shortly, glancing at Tyler.

Bella lifted her small chin. "He's not blind," she said. "He knows what goes on here."

"Take my pie back in the house," Nell told her.

Bella glared at her. "She's not getting a bite of it."

"Tell her."

The older woman nodded curtly. "Don't think I won't." She glanced at Tyler and grinned. "You can have a slice, though."

He took off his hat and bowed. "I'll eat every crumb twice."

She laughed gleefully and went back inside.

"Aren't you late for the camp out?" Nell asked curiously.

"We canceled it," he replied. "Mr. Curtis fell into a cactus and Mrs. Sims got sick on the chili we had at lunch and had to go to bed. The rest figured they'd rather watch television."

Nell smiled faintly. "Oh, well. The best laid plans . . . We'll try it again on the weekend."

Tyler studied her quietly, his eyes narrowed in thought. "About this afternoon . . ." he began, holding Nell's surprised gaze.

But before he could say another word, the door behind Nell swung open.

"Why, Tyler, how nice to see you again," Marguerite said laughingly, pausing in the doorway.

"Nice to see you again, Mrs. Regan," he replied dryly, and there was a world of knowledge in the pale green eyes that swept lazily down her slender body. Marguerite couldn't take him in with that strategic pose. He knew too much. But it was amusing to watch her try.

Nell wanted to throw herself down in the dust and cry, but that wouldn't have done any good. She went back inside, giving up without a struggle.

Marguerite gave her a curious glance, but Nell didn't even look at her. If she wanted Tyler, she was welcome to him, Nell thought miserably. After all, she had nothing to give him herself.

Supper was a quiet affair, except for the boys squabbling over everything from milk to beans.

"Tyler is taking me riding tomorrow," Marguerite said, giving Nell an apprehensive glance. "You'll mind the boys, won't you?"

Nell looked up. She felt rebellious. Restless. "As a matter of fact, I can't," she said with a faint smile. "Take them with you. Tyler's already said he wouldn't mind helping them find arrowheads."

"Sure!" Jess burst out. "I'd love to go."

"I'll go, too," Curt said.

Marguerite looked annoyed. "I don't want you along."

"You don't love us," Jess wailed.

"You never did," Curt seconded, and he started to cry.

Marguerite threw up her hands. "See what you've done now!" she accused Nell.

"I haven't done anything except refuse to be your doormat." Nell finished her potatoes. "I don't remember inviting you here," she replied coolly. "Don't expect me to entertain you or baby-sit for you."

"You always have before," Marguerite reminded her.

"That was before," Nell replied. "I'm not doing it anymore. You'll have to take care of yourself."

"Who's been talking to you?" Marguerite asked, fascinated.

"Nobody has," Nell replied. "I'm just tired of holding up the world. Why don't you get a job?"

Marguerite's gasp was audible, but Nell had gotten up and left the table before she had time for any outbursts.

* * *

Tyler took Marguerite and the boys riding the next morning. Marguerite did look good in a riding habit, Nell had to concede, but the redhead was obviously out of sorts at having the boys along. Tyler hadn't fussed about taking the boys, either. He liked children. Nell smiled. She liked them, too, but it was Marguerite's job to be their mother, not Nell's.

She wandered out to the kitchen and picked up a biscuit, having refused breakfast because she hadn't wanted to hear Margie raising cain about the boys going along on her romantic ride.

"And what's eating you, as if I didn't know?" Bella asked.

Nell laughed. "Nothing at all."

"You've got Margie running for cover. Imagine, you talking back to her and refusing to be pushed around. Are you sick or something?" she added, her keen old eyes probing.

Nell bit into the biscuit. "Not at all. I'm just tired of being worked to death, I guess."

"And watching Margie flirt with Tyler, I've no doubt."

Nell glared at the older woman. "Stop that. You know I don't like him."

"You like him. Maybe it's my fault that things never got going between you," Bella confessed gently. "I was trying to spare you more heartache, or I'd never have said anything when you put on that pretty dress...."

Nell turned away. She didn't like being reminded of that day. "He isn't my type," she said gruffly. "He's Margie's type."

"That's what you think," Bella murmured dryly. She put her towel down and stood staring at the other woman. "I've wanted to tell you for years that most men are nice critters. Some of them are even domesticated. All men aren't like Darren McAnders," she added, watching Nell's face go pale. "And he wasn't even that bad except when he was pushed into getting drunk. He loved Margie."

"And I loved him," Nell said coldly. "He flirted with me and teased me, just like Tyler did at first. And then he did...he did that to me, and it wasn't even because he was attracted to me. It was just to make Margie jealous!"

"It was despicable," Bella agreed. "But it was worse for you because you cared about him, and you felt betrayed and used. It was a good thing I happened upstairs when I did."

"Yes," Nell said tautly. The memories hurt.

"But it wasn't as bad as you've always made it out to be, either," Bella said firmly, ignoring the shocked look she got from Nell. "It wasn't," she added. "If you'd ever gone out with boys or had a date, you'd understand what happened a lot better. You hadn't even been kissed—"

"Stop it," Nell muttered miserably. She stuck her hands in her jeans and shifted. "It doesn't matter, anyway. I'm plain and countrified and no man is ever going to want me, no matter what I do. And I heard what Tyler said that night," she added with a cold glare. "I heard every word. He said he didn't want a 'lovesick tomboy hanging on to his boots.'"

Bella sighed. "So you did hear him. I was afraid that's why he was getting the deep-freeze treatment lately."

"It doesn't matter, you know," Nell said with deliberate carelessness. "It's just as well I found out early that I was annoying him. I've been careful not to bother him since."

Bella started to say something, but obviously thought better of it. "How long is Her Highness here for?"

"Just until tomorrow afternoon, thank God." Nell sighed. "I'd better get cracking. We're going riding, and then this afternoon I've got a busload of shoppers to take into town. I thought I'd run them over to the El Con mall. They might like to get some real Western gear at Cooper's."

"The silversmiths are over near San Xavier," she was reminded. "And they could have some Papago fry bread for refreshments."

"Tohono o'odham," Nell corrected automatically. "That's a real Papago word, meaning people of the desert. They changed it because they got tired of being called 'bean people' in Zuni."

"I can't say that," Bella muttered.

"Sure you can. *Tohono o'odham.* Anyway, the fry bread is a good idea if we have any time left from the shopping."

"Are any of the husbands tagging along?" Bella asked.

Nell pursed her lips. "Do you think I'd look this cheerful if the men were coming with us?"

"Stupid question," Bella said with a sigh. "I'd better get started on chow, or is Chappy laying on a barbecue tonight before the square dance? He never asks me, he just goes ahead with whatever he wants to do."

"Chappy did say something about a barbecue. Why don't you make a bowl of potato salad and some home-made rolls and a few pies to go with it?" She put an arm around Bella's formidable girth. "That will save you some work, too, won't it? Actually, I think Chappy's kind of sweet on you."

Bella flushed and glared at Nell. "He ain't, neither! Now get out of here and let me get busy."

"Yes, ma'am." Nell grinned and curtsied before she darted out the back door.

Nell went down to the stables to check on the mounts for the morning ride. Chappy Staples was alone there, and after all the years, Nell was still a little in awe of him. He was older than most of the men, but he could outride the best of them. He'd never said a thing out of the way to Nell, but she couldn't help her remoteness. It was the same with all the men, except Tyler.

"How is the mare this morning?" she asked the wiry man with the pale blue eyes, referring to a horse with a bad shoe.

"I had the farrier come over and take a look at her. He replaced the shoe, but she's still restless this morning. I wouldn't take her out if I were you."

She sighed. "That will leave us one mount short," she murmured. "Margie's gone riding with Tyler and the boys."

"If you can handle it alone, I'll keep Marlowe here and let him help me work the colt, and one of the guests can have his horse," Chappy said. "How about it?"

"That sounds great." She sighed, thanking her lucky stars that the foulmouthed Marlowe was being kept clear of her guests. If he kept it up, he'd have to go, and that would leave them a man short. Nell didn't like the idea of adding on new men. It had taken her long enough to get used to the ones she already had on the place.

"We'll start at ten," she told Chappy. "And we have to be back in time for lunch. I'm taking the ladies shopping about one-thirty."

"No problem, ma'am." He tipped his hat and returned to work.

Nell wandered back toward the house, deep in thought, almost running head-on into Tyler because she didn't see him until he rounded the corner of the house.

She gasped, stepping back. "Sorry," she said, faltering. "I didn't see you."

He glared down at her. "I was about to head off riding with Margie and the boys when I heard that I'm escorting Margie to the square dance tonight."

"Are you?" she asked, all at sea.

He lifted an eyebrow. "That's what Margie tells me. She said it was your idea," he added in an exaggerated Texas drawl that could have skinned a cactus at close range.

"I guess you wouldn't believe me if I told you I haven't said a word to her about it," she said resignedly.

"You throw her at me every time she comes out here, don't you?" he asked with a mocking smile.

She lowered her eyes and turned away. "I did once or twice, sure. I thought you might enjoy her company," she said in a subdued tone. "She's like you. Sophisticated and classy and upper crust. But if you'd rather she went with someone else, I'll see what I can do."

He caught her arm, noticing the way she tensed and froze. "All right. You don't have to make a federal case out of it. I just don't like having myself volunteered for guest escort services. I like Margie, but I don't need a matchmaker."

"No, you wouldn't," she said more sadly than she realized. "Will you let go of my arm, please?"

"You can't bear to be touched, can you?" he asked speculatively. "That was one of the first things I noticed about you. Why?"

Her heart went wild. He couldn't know that it was his touch lancing through her like white-hot pleasure that made her tremble, not a dislike of being touched by him. And that surprised her. "My private life is none of your business," she said firmly.

"No. You've made that very clear lately," he replied. He let her go as if her arm burned his fingers. "Okay, honey. Have it your own way. As for Margie, I'll work things out with her."

He sounded vaguely exasperated, but Nell was far too nervous to wonder about his tone of voice. A quick get-away was on her mind. When she was alone with him, it took all her willpower not to throw herself into his arms, despite all her inhibitions.

"Okay," she said, and shrugged, as if what he did were of no consequence to her. She went around him and into the house without looking back, unaware of his quiet gaze following her every step of the way.

Chapter Two

Nell avoided Tyler for the rest of the day, and she didn't go to the square dance that night. She excused herself right after the barbecue and went up to her room. She was being a coward, she thought miserably, but at least she wouldn't have to watch Margie flirt with Tyler.

But memories of Tyler wouldn't be put out of her mind. Her thoughts drifted relentlessly back to the very beginning, to his first few days at the ranch. From the moment she'd met him at the airport, he'd been gentle and kind to her, putting her at ease, making himself right at home in her company.

And not only with Nell—he'd won over the men and Bella just as quickly. Nell had warmed to him as she never had to any man, with the exception of Darren Mc-Anders. But even though Darren had left deep scars on her emotions, Nell knew instinctively that Tyler wouldn't harm her. Before she realized what was happening to her, she was following him around like a puppy.

She grimaced, remembering. She'd alternated between sighing over him and trying to find ways to make him more comfortable. She didn't realize how her eagerness to please him might seem to other people . . . or even to Tyler. She was in awe of him, the wound of McAnders's long-ago rejection forgotten.

There was a square dance the second week he was in residence. Nell hadn't put on a dress, but she did make sure her long hair was clean and neatly brushed, and she didn't wear her slouch hat. As usual when there were strangers around, especially male ones, she drew into herself. Tyler made a convenient hiding place, and she got behind him and stayed there.

"Scared?" he'd teased gently, not minding her shy company. She was a little sunflower, a child to cosset. He hadn't asked her age, but he assumed she hadn't made it out of her teens yet. She didn't threaten him in any way, and he could afford to be kind to her.

"I don't mix well," she confessed, smiling. "And I don't really trust men very much. Some of the guests . . . well, they're older men and their wives aren't interested in them. I guess any young woman, even one like me, is fair game to them. I don't want trouble, so mostly I stay away from dances." Her dark eyes sought his. "You don't mind if I stick back here with you?"

"Of course not." He leaned against one of the posts that supported the loft and busied his fingers braiding three strands of rawhide he'd found. "I haven't been to a barn dance in a long time. Is this an ongoing ritual here?"

"Every other Saturday night," she confided. "We even invite the kids, so everybody gets to join in. The band—" she indicated the four-man band "—is a local group. We pay them forty dollars for the evening. They aren't famous, but we think they're pretty good."

"They are," he agreed with a smile. He glanced down at her, wondering what she'd think of the kind of party he was used to, where the women wore designer gowns and there were full orchestras or at least string quartets and jazz quintets to provide the music.

She twisted a strand of her hair in her fingers nervously, watching the married couples dance. There was a wistful expression in her eyes. He frowned as he watched her.

"Do you want to dance, Nell?" he asked gently.

She blushed. "No. I, well, I don't dance," she confessed, thrilling to the thought of being in his arms. But that might not be a good thing. He might see how attracted she was to him. She felt helpless when his hand accidentally brushed hers. She wasn't sure she could handle a dose of him at close quarters without giving away her growing infatuation for him.

"I could teach you," he volunteered, faintly amused at her reticence.

"No, I'd better not. I don't want to…" She was going to say that she didn't want to have to explain to the male guests why she wouldn't dance with anyone but Tyler. It was too hard to make him understand that her flesh crawled at the thought of being handled by strange hands. But she coveted *his* touch, and that was new.

"Okay, tidbit. No need to worry the point." He smiled. "But I think I'm about to be abducted, so what will you do while I'm away?" he asked, indicating a heavyset middle-aged woman who was heading toward him with a gleeful smile.

"I'll just help out at the refreshment table," she said, and excused herself. She watched him being led onto the dance floor and she sighed, wishing she was the one dancing with the long, tall Texan. But she was uncertain of herself. It was better if she didn't rush things. Much better.

After that evening, he became her port in a storm. If there were business meetings or problems that she had to discuss with the men or male guests, she always made sure Tyler was included. She began to think of him as a buffer between herself and a world that frightened her. But even as she relied on him, she couldn't help feeling an attraction that was making it impossible for her to go on as she had. She wanted him to notice her, to see her as a woman. It was the first time in years that she'd wanted to show off her femininity, to look the way a woman should.

But as she stared at herself in her mirror one morning, she wanted to cry. There wasn't even good raw material to work with. She'd seen photos of movie stars who looked almost as bad as she did without their makeup, but she didn't have the first idea how to make herself look beautiful. Her hair, while long and lustrous, needed shaping. Her eyebrows almost disappeared because they were so sun bleached. She had a good figure, but she was too shy to wear revealing clothes. Maybe it wasn't a good idea to go overboard, anyway, she told herself. It had taken years to get over her bad experience and the brutal honesty of the first man she'd set her cap at.

Finally, she'd braided her hair into two long pigtails and looped Indian beaded holders around them. That didn't look too bad, considering that her paternal grandmother was a full-blooded Apache. She only wished her face looked as good as her hair did. Well, miracles did happen. Maybe someday one would happen for her. And Tyler did actually seem to like her.

She tried a hint of lipstick and put on her newest jeans—the only ones she had that really fit properly—with a pullover knit blouse. She smiled at her reflection. She really didn't look too bad, she thought, except for her face. Maybe she could wear a gunnysack over it....

Then Bella called her to lunch before she had time to worry anymore.

She bounced into the dining room with more energy than she'd had for weeks. She felt reborn, full of new, shy confidence. She was blooming.

The rain had come to the desert, making the guests uncomfortable and ranching dangerous. The men were working overtime keeping cattle and horses out of the dry washes that could kill so suddenly and efficiently when they filled with unexpected rainwater. The past three days had brought a deluge, and two of the guests were giving up and going home. The other eight were going to tough it out. Nell had smiled at their stubbornness and was determined to make life as pleasant as possible for them.

The guests were having their meal half an hour later than Nell, Tyler and Bella in the huge oak-decorated dining room with its heavy chairs and table and comfortable lounge furniture.

Tyler hadn't shown up, but Bella was bustling around putting platters of food on the table when she got a glimpse of the mistress of the house and almost dropped the tray she was carrying.

"That you, Nell?" she asked hesitantly, her gray head cocked sideways.

"Who are you expecting?" Nell asked, laughing. "Well, I won't win any beauty contests, but don't I look better?"

"Too much better," Bella said gently. "Oh, honey, don't do it. Don't set yourself up for such a hard fall."

Nell stopped breathing. "What?" she asked.

"You take him things for the cabin," Bella said. "You sew buttons on his shirts. You make sure he's warm and dry when it rains. You're forever making him special things in the kitchen. And now this transformation. Honey, he's a sophisticated man who was, until just recently, very rich and well traveled." She looked worried. "I don't want to smash any dreams, but he's used to a different kind of woman. He's being kind to you, Nell. But that's all it is. Don't mistake kindness for true love. Not again."

Nell's face went bloodred. She hadn't realized that she was doing those things. She'd liked him and she wanted him to be happy. But it didn't look like that—of course it didn't. And her new appearance was going to put him in a very embarrassing situation.

"I like him," Nell faltered. "But I'm not . . . not chasing him." She turned and ran upstairs. "I'll change."

"Nell!"

She ignored Bella's remorseful wail and kept going. But she wouldn't come back down for dinner, despite the pleading from the other side of the door. She felt raw and hurt, even though Bella had just meant to be kind. Nell was going to have to watch her step. She couldn't afford to let Tyler think she was chasing him. God forbid that she should invite heartache again.

Downstairs, Tyler and Bella had been sharing a quiet meal. He studied the old woman curiously.

"Something bothering you?" he asked politely.

"Nell." She sighed. "She won't come down. She fixed her hair and changed clothes, and I . . ." She cleared her throat. "I said something."

"Nell could use a little self-confidence," Tyler said quietly. "That wasn't kind of you to knock her down when she was just getting started."

"I don't want her to get hurt again," Bella moaned. "You just mean to be kind, I know that. But that child has never had any affection, except from me. She doesn't know what it is to be loved and wanted. Her father lived for Ted. Nell was always an afterthought. And the only other time she was interested in a man, she got hurt bad." She sighed again. "So maybe I'm overprotective. But I just didn't want to see her throw herself at you because you pay her a little attention."

"I never thought she was," Tyler said, smiling. "You're wrong. Nell's just being friendly. She's a cute little kid with pretty brown eyes and a nice way about her. I like her and she likes me. But that's all it is. You don't have to worry."

Bella eyed him, wondering if he could be that blind. Maybe he could. "Nell is twenty-four," she said.

His black eyebrows arched. "I beg your pardon?"

"Well, how old did you think she was?" the woman asked.

"Nineteen. Eighteen, maybe." He frowned. "Are you serious?"

"Never more so," Bella told him. "So please don't make the mistake of putting her in patent leather shoes and ruffled pinafores. She's a grown woman who's lived alone and been slighted all her life. She's just ripe to have her heart torn out by the roots. Please don't be the one to do that to her."

Tyler hardly heard her. He'd thought of Nell as a cute kid, but maybe he'd gotten everything wrong. Surely she didn't see him as a potential romantic interest? That was just too farfetched. Why, she wasn't even his type. He preferred a much more sophisticated, worldly woman.

He picked at his food. "I didn't realize," he began, "that she might be thinking of me in those terms. I'll make sure I don't do anything to encourage her." He smiled at Bella. "I sure as hell don't want a lovesick tomboy grabbing me by the boots every time I walk by. I don't like being chased, even by attractive women. And Nell is a sweet child, but even a blind man couldn't accuse her of being beautiful."

"Have some more beef," Bella said after a minute, grateful that Nell was still up in her room and not likely to hear what he'd said.

Of course, as fate would have it, Nell had started back down the hall and was standing just outside the door. She'd heard every word, and her face was a pasty white. She just barely made it back to her room before the tears that she'd pent-up escaped.

Maybe it had been for the best that she'd found out early what Tyler really thought of her. She'd gone a little crazy because of the attention he'd paid her, but now that she knew what he really felt about her, she'd keep those stupid impulses under better control. Like Bella said, she'd mistaken kindness for interest. And she should have known better. For God's sake, hadn't she learned her lesson already? She had nothing that would attract a man.

So she'd dried her eyes and put back on her comfortable clothes, and later she'd gone down to supper as if nothing at all had happened. Neither Bella nor Tyler realized what she'd overheard, and she hadn't told them.

But after learning how Tyler felt, Nell's attitude toward him changed. She was polite and helpful, but the light that had been in her eyes when she looked at him had gone out. She never looked directly at him and she never sought him out. The little attentions vanished, as did her shy adoration. She treated him like any other ranch hand, and what she really felt, only she knew. She never talked about him again, even to Bella.

But tonight, in the silence of her room, she still ached for what might have been. It seemed very likely that she wasn't cut out for a close relationship with a man, much less with Tyler Jacobs. But that didn't stop her from being hurt by what had happened. It had been the first time in years that she'd made an effort to look like a woman. It would be the last, too, she vowed. She rolled over and closed her eyes. Minutes later, she was asleep.

A couple of weeks later, the sun was out, thank God, because the recent rains had been catastrophic. Bookings had been canceled and the ranch's finances had suffered. But now they had all eighteen rooms filled, most of them double occupancy. The ranch catered to families with children, and family fun was emphasized, with hayrides and trail rides and barbecues and square dancing. They did a lot of repeat business. Mr. Howes and his wife had been regulars for ten years, and although Mr. Howes spent a great deal of his time falling off his horse, it never seemed to deter him from trying to keep his girth in the saddle. And despite the fact that Mrs. Sims had been infuriating her ulcer with Crowbait's homemade firehouse chili for the past five years, she kept trying to eat it. She was a widow who taught school back East during the year and vacationed for a week at the ranch every summer.

Most of the regulars were like family now, and even the husbands didn't bother Nell because she knew them. But there was always the exception, like the very greasy-looking Mr. Cova who had a plain, loving wife whose affection he seemed determined to abuse. He was always watching Nell, and she looked forward to the day when they left.

"You could have Tyler speak to Mr. Cova, if things get too rough," Bella mentioned as she was setting the buffet table for lunch.

"No, thanks," Nell said quietly. "I can take care of myself."

She turned, almost colliding with Tyler's tall form as he appeared quietly in the doorway. She mumbled an apology and dashed past him without a word. He watched her irritably for a minute before he swung himself into a straddling position over one of the kitchen chairs and tossed his hat onto the table. His lean, dark hands lit a cigarette while he nursed a warm regret for the friendliness he'd once shared with Nell. He felt as if he'd hurt her somehow. Her quiet sensitivity disturbed him. She touched a chord in him that no other woman had ever reached.

"You're brooding again," Bella murmured dryly.

He smiled faintly. "It's just that Nell's changed," he said quietly, lifting the cigarette to his chiseled lips. "I thought we were going to be the best of friends. But now, when I come into a room, she can't leave quick enough. She sends me messages through Chappy. If I need to see the books, she has somebody bring them to me." He shrugged. "I feel like a damned leper."

"She's just nervous around men," Bella soothed. "She always has been—ask Chappy."

Tyler's green eyes shifted and met hers. "It wasn't like this at first. I couldn't turn around without bumping into her. Do you know why things changed?"

Bella shrugged. "If I did," she said, choosing her words carefully, "she wouldn't thank me for saying anything. Although she sure is quiet these days."

"Amen. Well, maybe it's just as well," Tyler murmured absently. He took a draw from his cigarette. "What's for lunch?"

"Open-faced roast beef sandwiches, homemade French fries, salad, homemade banana pudding and iced tea and coffee."

"Sounds delicious. By the way, I've added two new men on the payroll to help do some work on the equipment and renovate the stable and the barn. That's going to have to be done before we finish haying, as I'm sure you know."

Bella whistled through her teeth. "Nell isn't going to like that. She hates having to deal with new men."

He scowled at her. "What happened to her?"

"I can't tell you that. She'll have to."

"I've asked, but all I got was the runaround."

"She's a secretive person. Nell doesn't talk about herself, and I won't." She smiled to soften the words. "Trusting someone doesn't come easy to that child."

"Trust is difficult for most of us." He tilted his hat over his eyes. "See you."

The barn, like every other building on the place, leaked in heavy rain, but when it was sunny like today, it was cozy and plenty warm enough. Nell was kneeling beside a small Hereford calf in a rickety stall filled with green-gold hay, stroking its head.

Tyler stood in the hay-filled aisle watching her for a long moment, his eyes narrowed in thought. She looked like Orphan Annie, and maybe she felt that way. He knew what it was like to live without love, to be alone and alienated. He understood her, but she wouldn't let him close enough to tell her so. He'd made a mistake with Nell. He didn't even know what he'd done to make her back off and treat him with such cool indifference. He missed the way things had been at their first meeting. Her shy adoration had touched him, warmed him. Because of Nell, he felt a kind of emptiness that he didn't even understand.

He moved closer, watching the way she reacted to his approach, the way her dark eyes fell, her quick movements as she got to her feet and moved out into the aisle. As if, he thought irritably, she couldn't bear being in an enclosed space with him.

"I thought I'd better tell you that I've hired two men, temporarily, to help with some repairs," he said. "Don't panic," he added when he saw the flash of fear in her eyes. "They're not ax murderers, and they won't try to rape you."

She blushed furiously and tears burned her eyes. She didn't say a word. She turned and stormed out of the barn, hurting in ways she couldn't have told him about, old memories blazing up like bonfires in the back of her mind.

"Damn it—!" he burst out angrily. He was one step behind her. Even as she reached the barn door, he caught her arm firmly to stop her. The reaction he got shocked him.

She cried out, twisting sharply away from him, her eyes wide and dark and fearful.

He realized belatedly that what had frightened her was the anger in his face, the physical expression of it in his firm hold on her. "I don't hit women," he said quietly, moving back a step. "And I didn't mean to upset you. I shouldn't have made that crack about the new men. Nell..."

She swallowed, stuffing her hands into her jeans while she fought for composure. She hated letting him see the fear his violence had incited. She glanced away from him and her thick black lashes blocked his view of the emotion in her dark eyes.

He moved closer, looming over her. His lean hands slid into the thick coolness of her hair at her ears and tilted her face up to his.

"Stop running," he said curtly. "You've done it for weeks, and I can't take much more. I can't get near you."

"I don't want you near me," she said, choking on the words. "Let go."

Her words stung his pride, but he didn't let her see. "Tell me why, then," he persisted. His gaze was level, unblinking. "Come on."

"I heard what you said to Bella that night," she said, averting her eyes. "You thought I was just a kid, and when she told you how old I really was, you... you said you didn't want a tomboy hanging from your boots," she whispered huskily.

He saw the tears before he felt them sliding onto the backs of his hands. "So that was it." He grimaced. He hadn't realized that Nell might have heard him. His words must have cut her to the quick. "Nell, I never meant for you to hear me," he said gently.

"It was a good thing," she said, lifting her chin proudly as she fought down embarrassment. "I didn't realize how... how silly I was behaving. I won't embarrass you anymore, I promise. I liked you, that was all. I wanted you to be happy here." She laughed huskily. "I know I'm not the kind of girl who would appeal to a man like you, and I wasn't throwing myself at you." Her eyes closed on a wave of pain. "Now, please, will you let me go?"

"Oh, Nell," he groaned. He pulled her close, wrapping her up in his arms, his dark head bent to her honey-brown one under the slouch hat. He rocked her, feeling the pain in her as if it hurt him, too. His eyes closed as he swung her in his arms, the close contact easing the tears, easing the pain. She wept silently at the sweetness of it, even while she knew that she couldn't expect any more than this. A few seconds of pity mingled with guilt. Cold comfort for a lonely life.

She let herself rest against him for one exquisite moment, loving the wiry strength of his tall body, the leather and tobacco smells that clung to his soft cotton shirt, the sound of his heartbeat under her ear. This would be something to dream about when he left. But now, she had to be strong.

She pulled away from him and he let her go. She knew that there was no hope for her in his life. Margie was more like him—she was sophisticated and good-looking and mature. They'd hit it off like a house on fire, and Nell had to keep that in mind and not let her heart get addicted to Tyler. Because Margie wanted him, Nell was sure of it. And Margie always got what she wanted.

She drew in a shaky breath. "Thanks for the comfort," she said. She even forced a smile. "You don't have to worry about me. I won't make things hard for you." She looked up, her brown eyes very soft and dark, shimmering with a hurt that she was trying so hard to keep from him.

Tyler felt something stir in him that knocked him in the knees. She had the most beautiful, sensual eyes he'd ever seen. They made him hungry, but for things that had no physical expression. She made him feel as if he'd been out in the cold all his life, and there was a warm fire waiting for him.

Nell felt that hunger in him, but she was afraid of it. His eyes had become a glittering green, and they were so intent that she flushed and dropped her gaze to his chest. He made her weak all over. If he looked at her like that very often, she'd have to go off into the desert forever. She felt as if he were taking possession of her without a physical move.

She stepped back, nervous, unsure of herself. "I'd better go inside."

"About those new men—they're only temporary. Just until we get through roundup." His voice sounded oddly strained. He lit a cigarette, surprised to find that his fingers were unsteady. "They'll be here in a few weeks."

She managed a shy smile. "Well, I'll try not to treat them like ax murderers," she promised nervously. "I'm sorry about the square dance. About leaving you to deal with Margie." She lifted her shoulders jerkily.

"I don't mind. But don't make a habit of it, okay?" he asked, smiling to soften the words. He reached out and tugged a lock of her long, unruly hair. "I'm feeling a little raw right now, Nell. I've lost my home, my job...everything that used to matter. I'm still trying to find my feet. There's no place in my life for a woman just yet."

"I'm sorry about what you lost, Tyler," she said with genuine sincerity, gazing up at his hard, dark face. "But you'll get it all back one day. You're that kind of person. I can't see you giving up and settling for weekly wages."

He smiled slowly, surprised at her perception. "Can't you? You're no quitter yourself, little Nell."

She blushed. "I'm not little."

He moved a step closer with a new kind of slowness, a sensual kind of movement that made Nell's heart stop and then skip wildly. She could barely breathe, the manly cologne he wore drifting into her nostrils, seducing her. "You're not very big, either," he mused. He touched the very visible pulse in her soft neck, tracing it with a long, teasing finger that made it jump. "Nervous, honey?" he breathed.

She could hardly find enough breath to answer him. "I . . . I have to go inside."

His head bent so that his green eyes were looking straight into her dark ones while that maddening finger traced a hot path down her throat and up to her jaw. "Do you?" he asked in a husky whisper, and his breath touched her parted lips like a kiss.

"Tyler . . ." Odd, how different her voice sounded. Strained. Almost frantic.

His eyes fell to her mouth, and he wanted it suddenly and fiercely. His chest rose and fell quickly, his eyes glittered down at her. He almost bent that scant inch that would have brought her soft, full mouth under his. But she was trembling, and he couldn't be sure that it wasn't from fear. It was too soon. Much too soon.

He forced himself to draw back, but his hand gripped her shoulder tightly before he let her go. "See you later," he said with a slow smile.

She cleared her throat. For one wild second, she'd thought he meant to kiss her, but that was absurd. "Sure," she said huskily. "See you."

She turned and went into the house on wobbly legs. She was going to have to get her imagination under con-

trol. Tyler was only teasing, just as he had in the beginning. At least he still liked her. If she could control her
foolish heart, they might yet become friends. She could
hardly hope for anything more, with Margie around.

Chapter Three

A couple of weekends later, Margie and the boys were back at the ranch. Curt and Jess were up at the crack of dawn Sunday, and Nell noticed with faint humor that they followed Tyler wherever he went. That gave Margie a good excuse to tag along, too, but the woman seemed preoccupied. She'd tried to get a conversation going with Nell earlier, although Nell hadn't been forthcoming. It was hard going, listening to Margie try to order her life for her. Margie apparently hadn't noticed that her sister-in-law was a capable adult. She spent most of her time at the ranch trying to change Nell into the kind of person she wanted her to be. Or so it seemed to Nell.

"I do wish you'd let me fix your face and help you buy some new clothes," Margie grumbled at the breakfast table. She glared at Nell's usual attire. "And you might as well wear a gunnysack as that old outfit. You'd get just as much notice from the men, anyway."

"I don't want the men to notice me," Nell replied tersely.

"Well, you should," she said stubbornly. "That incident was a long time ago, Nell," she added with a fixed stare, "and not really as traumatic as you've made it out to be. And don't argue," she added when Nell bristled. "You were just a child, at a very impressionable age, and you'd had a crush on Darren. I'm not saying that you invited it, because we both know you didn't. But it's time you faced what a relationship really is between a man and a woman. You can't be a little girl forever."

"I'm not a little girl," Nell said through her teeth. She knew her cheeks were scarlet. "And I know what relationships are. I don't happen to want one."

"You should. You're going to wind up an old maid, and it's a pitiful waste." Margie folded her arms over the low bodice of her white peasant dress with its graceful flounces and ruffles. "Look, honey," she began, her voice softening, "I know it was mostly my fault. I'm sorry. But you can't let it ruin your whole life. You've never talked to me or to Bella. I wish you had, because we could have helped you."

"I don't need help," Nell said icily.

"Yes, you do," Margie persisted. "You've got to stop hiding from life—"

"There you are," Tyler said, interrupting Margie's tirade. "Your offspring have cornered a bull snake out in the yard. Curt says you won't mind if he keeps it for a pet."

Margie looked up, horrified.

Tyler chuckled at the expression on her face. "Okay. I'll make him turn it loose." He glanced at Nell, noticing the way she averted her eyes and toyed nervously with her coffee cup. "Some of the guests are going to services. I thought I'd drive them. I'm partial to a good sermon.''

"Okay. Thanks," Nell said, ignoring Margie's obvious surprise.

"Did you think I was the walking image of sin?" Tyler asked the prettier woman. "Sorry to put a stick in your spokes, but I'm still just a country boy from Texas, despite the life-style I used to boast."

"My, my." Margie shook her head amusedly. "The mind boggles." She darted a glance at Nell, sitting like a rock. "You ought to take Nell along. She and her hair shirt would probably enjoy it."

"I don't wear a hair shirt, and I can drive myself to church later." Nell got up and left the room, her stiff back saying more than words.

She did go to church, to the late morning service, in a plain gray dress that did nothing for her, with no makeup on and her honey-brown hair in a neat bun. She looked as she lived—plainly. Bella had driven her to town and was going to pick her up when the service was over. It would have been the last straw to go earlier with Tyler's group, especially after Margie's infuriating invitation at Tyler's expense.

So the last person she expected to find waiting for her was Tyler, in a neat gray suit, lounging against the ranch station wagon at the front of the church when services were over.

"Where's Bella?" Nell asked bluntly.

Tyler raised a dark eyebrow. "Now, now," he chided gently. "It's Sunday. And I'd hate to let you walk back to the ranch."

"Bella was supposed to pick me up," she said, refusing to move.

"No sense in letting her come all this way when I had to come back to town anyway, was there?" he asked reasonably.

She eyed him warily. "Why did you have to make two trips to town on Sunday?"

"To pick you up, of course. Get in."

It wasn't as if she had a choice. He escorted her to the passenger side and put her in like so much laundry, closing the door gently behind her.

"You're killing my ego," he remarked as he pulled out onto the road.

Her nervous hands twisted her soft gray leather purse. "You don't have an ego," she replied, glancing out at the expanse of open country and jagged mountains.

"Thank you," he replied, smiling faintly. "That's the first nice thing you've said to me in weeks."

She let out a quiet breath and stared at the purse in her hands. "I don't mean to be like this," she confessed. "It's just—" her shoulders lifted and fell "—I don't want you to think that I'm running after you." She grimaced. "After all, I guess I was pretty obnoxious those first days you were here."

He pulled the station wagon onto a pasture trail that led beyond a locked gate, and cut off the engine. His green eyes lanced over her while he lit a cigarette with slow, steady hands.

"Okay, let's put our cards on the table," he said quietly. "I'm flat busted. I work for your uncle because what I have left in the bank wouldn't support me for a week, and I can't save a lot. I've got debts that I'm trying to pay off. That makes me a bad prospect for a woman. I'm not looking for involvement..."

She groaned, torn by embarrassment, and fumbled her way out of the car, scarlet with humiliated pride.

He was one step behind, and before she could get away he was in front of her, the threat of his tall, fit body holding her back against the station wagon.

"Please, you don't have to explain anything to me," she said brokenly. "I'm sorry, I never meant to—"

"Nell."

The sound of her name in that deep, slow drawl brought her hurt eyes up to his. Through a mist of gathering tears she saw his face harden, then his eyes begin to glitter again, as they had once before when he'd come close to her.

"You're all too vulnerable," he said, and there was something solemn and very adult in his look. "I'm trying to tell you that I never thought you were chasing me. You aren't the type."

She could have laughed at that statement. He didn't know that years ago she'd run shamelessly after Darren McAnders and almost begged for his love. But she didn't speak. Her eyes fell to the quick rise and fall of his broad chest under the well-fitting suit, and she wondered why he seemed so breathless. Her own breathing was much too quick, because he was close enough that she could feel his warmth, smell the expensive cologne that clung to him.

"I'm nervous around men," she said without looking up. "You were the first one who ever paid me any real attention. I guess I was so flattered that I went overboard, trying to make you happy here." She smiled faintly, glancing up and then down again. "But I never really thought it was anything except friendship on your part, you know. I'm not at all like Margie."

"What do you mean by that crack?" he asked sharply.

She shivered at his tone. "She's like the people in your world, that's all. She's poised and sophisticated and beautiful..."

"There are many different kinds of beauty, Nell," he said, his voice softer than she'd ever heard it. With surprised pleasure she felt the touch of his lean fingers on her chin as he lifted her face up to his eyes. "It goes a lot deeper than makeup."

Her lips parted and she found that she couldn't quite drag her eyes away from his. He was watching her in a way that made her knees weak.

"We'd better go...hadn't we?" she asked in a husky whisper.

The timbre of her soft voice sent ripples down his spine. He searched her dark eyes slowly, finding secrets there, unvoiced longings. He could almost feel the loneliness in her, the hidden need.

And all at once, he felt a need spark within him to erase that pain from her soft eyes.

He dropped his cigarette absently to the ground and put it out with a sharp movement of his boot. His lean hands slid against her high cheekbones and past her ears.

"Tyler...!" she gasped.

"Shhhhhh." He eased her back until she was resting against the station wagon, with his chest touching her taut breasts, and all the time his eyes searched hers, locked with them, binding her to him.

Her nervous hands, purse and all, pressed against him, but not with any real protest, and he knew it. This close, she couldn't hide her hunger from him.

"But..." she began.

"Nell." He whispered her name just as his lips brushed against hers. It wasn't a kiss at all. It was a breath of shivery sensation against her mouth, a tentative touch

that made her stand very still, because she was afraid that
he might stop if she moved.

His fingers toyed at her nape as they removed the
hairpins and loosened her hair, and all the while his
mouth was teasing hers, keeping her in thrall to him. He
closed one of her hands around her hairpins and ran his
fingers slowly through the mass of honey-streaked hair
he'd loosened, enjoying its silky coolness.

"Open your mouth a little," he whispered as his teeth
closed gently on her lower lip.

She blushed, but she obeyed him without pause.

His own mouth parted, and she watched it fit itself exactly to the contours of her lips. Her eyes glanced off his
fiery ones, and then the sensation began to penetrate her
shocked nerves, and she gasped as her eyes closed in
aching pleasure.

He murmured something deep and rough, and then she
felt the length of his hard body easing down against hers
while birds called in the meadow and an airplane flew
overhead and the sun beat down on her head. She
moaned in sweet oblivion.

He felt her tremble, heard the first cry from her lips.
His mouth lifted just enough for him to see her face, and
he was startled by the pleasure he found there. Her eyes
opened, black pools of velvet. His hands slid gently down
her back to her waist, and he realized that breathing had
become an Olympic event.

"My God," he whispered, but with reverence, because not once in his life had he felt this overwhelming
tenderness for a woman.

"You...you shouldn't hold me...like this," she
whispered back, her voice shattering with mingled fear
and need.

"Why not?" He brushed his nose against hers while he spoke and managed a faint smile for her.

She colored. "You know why not."

"No, I don't." His mouth covered hers slowly, and he felt her yield, felt her submission like a drug as he drowned in the softness of her body and the sweetness of her mouth. He relaxed, giving in to his own need. His hips slowly pressed against hers, letting her feel what she probably already knew... that he was feverishly aroused by her.

She stiffened and gasped, and without warning he felt her ardor turn to fear as she pushed at his chest in flaming embarrassment.

He drew away gently, releasing her from the soft crush of his body. His eyes searched her scarlet face, noting the way she kept her own eyes hidden.

"You haven't done this before," he said with sudden conviction.

"Not... not voluntarily, no," she replied with forced lightness. She gnawed on her lip. "I'm sorry. It's... it's a little scary." And she blushed again, even more.

He laughed softly, delighted. His mouth pressed gently against her forehead. He nuzzled her face with his. "I suppose it would be, to a quiet little virgin who doesn't chase men."

"Please don't make fun of me," she whispered.

"Was that how it sounded?" He lifted his head, touching her mouth with a slow, tender forefinger as he watched her. "I didn't mean it to. I'm not used to innocents, Nell. The world I came from didn't accept them very readily."

"Oh. I see."

"No, you don't, honey. And that's a good thing. It isn't my world any longer. I'm not sure I even miss it."

He toyed with a long, silky strand of her hair. "You're trembling," he whispered.

"I'm...this is...it's new."

"It's new for me, too, although I imagine you don't believe it." He brushed the hair back from her face, and his green eyes searched her dark ones. "How long is it since a man kissed you...really kissed you?"

"I don't think anyone ever did, and meant it," she confessed.

"Why?"

"I don't attract men," she faltered.

"Really?" He smiled but without mirth as he caught her by the waist and pulled her to him. She flushed and tried to pull away, but this time he held her firmly.

"Tyler!" she protested, flustered.

"Just stand still," he said quietly, but he let her hips pull away without an argument. "You're twenty-four years old and damned ignorant about men. It's time you had a little instruction. I won't hurt you, but I can't kiss you from a safe distance."

"You shouldn't," she pleaded, looking up. "It isn't fair to...to play with me."

His dark eyes didn't blink. "Is that what I'm doing, Nell?" he asked softly. "Am I playing?"

"What else could you be doing?"

"What else, indeed," he breathed as his head bent. He pulled her up to meet the hard descent of his mouth, and he kissed her with passion and a little anger, because she was arousing him in ways she couldn't have dreamed. He couldn't stop what was happening, and that irritated him even more. Nell was the last woman in the world he should be kissing this way. He had no right to get involved with her when he had nothing to offer. But her mouth was sweet and gentle under his, softly parting; her body, after its first resistance, melting into his. He lifted her against his chest, drowning in the long, sweet, aching pleasure of the most chaste kiss he'd ever shared with a woman. His body fairly throbbed against her, but he kept himself in full control. This was an interlude that couldn't end in a bedroom; he had to remember that.

He groaned finally and listened to reason. He put her back on her feet, his hands gripping her soft arms hard as he held her in front of him and struggled for both breath and sanity.

Nell was dazed. Her eyes searched his glittery ones, and she could feel the fine tremor in his hands as he held her. He was breathing as roughly as she was. He wanted her. She knew it suddenly and without a doubt. With a sense of shock, she realized how much a man he really was.

"I need to sit down," she said shakily.

"I'm just that unsteady myself, if you want the truth," he said on a rough sigh. He opened the door and let her into the station wagon before he slid his long legs inside and got in under the wheel.

He lit a cigarette and sat quietly, not speaking, while Nell fumbled her hairpins into her purse and dug out a small brush to run through her long, disheveled hair. She would have liked to check her appearance in a mirror, but that would look suspicious. She didn't want him to know how desperately sweet that interlude had been for her.

She put the brush back into her purse and closed it and stared down into her lap. Now that it was all over, she wondered how he felt. Would he think she was that starved for affection that she'd have reacted the same way to any man? She glanced at him nervously, but he seemed oblivious to her presence. He was staring out the windshield, apparently deep in thought.

In fact, he was trying to breathe normally. It was unusual for him to feel so shaken by such an innocent kiss. He couldn't remember the last time a woman had thrown him off balance. But Nell seemed to do it effortlessly, and that bothered him. Loss of control was the last thing he could afford with a virgin. He had to put on the brakes, and fast. The question was, how was he going to do that without making Nell think that he was little more than a playboy having fun?

He turned his head and found her watching the landscape without any particular expression on her soft face.

"We'll be late for lunch," Nell remarked without looking at him. She couldn't. She was too embarrassed by her reaction to his kiss.

He searched for the right words to explain what had happened, but Nell was far too unsophisticated for that kind of discussion. She seemed remarkably naive in a number of ways. He imagined her own abandon had been as embarrassing to her as his lack of control had been disturbing to him.

Better to let things lie, he supposed, for the time being. He started the station wagon without another word and headed for the ranch.

Margie got the boys ready to go early in the afternoon, and Tyler volunteered to take them back to Tucson. That seemed to thrill Margie, and it was a relief to Nell, who'd dreaded being alone with her sister-in-law. Margie had a way of dragging information out of her, and Nell didn't want to share what had happened with Tyler. It was a secret. A sweet, very private secret, which she was going to live on for a long time.

"You're not brooding again, are you?" Bella asked that evening as they washed supper dishes.

Nell shook her head. "No. I'm just grateful for a little peace. Margie was on her soapbox again about gussying me up." She sighed. "I don't think I'd like being a fashion plate, even if I had the raw material. I like me the way I am."

"Frumpy," Bella agreed.

She glared at the housekeeper. Nell's soapy hands lifted out of the water. "Look who's talking about frumpy!"

Bella glared back. "I ain't frumpy." She shifted her stance and shook back her wild silvery-black hair. "I'm unique."

Nell couldn't argue with that. "Okay, I give up. I'm frumpy."

"You could do with a little improvement. Maybe Margie isn't the terror we think she is. You know, she does care about you, in her way. She's only trying to help."

"She's trying to help herself into a relationship with Tyler," Nell corrected.

"She's lonely," Bella said. Her knowing eyes sought Nell's suddenly vulnerable face. "Aren't you?"

Nell stared at the soapsuds. "I think most people are," she said slowly. "And I guess Tyler could do worse. At least Margie makes him smile."

"You could, if you'd get that chip off your shoulder."

"I got hurt," Nell muttered.

"That's no reason to bury yourself. You're just twenty-four. You've got a lot of years left to be alone if you don't turn around pretty soon. You don't gain anything if you're afraid to take a chance. That isn't any way for a young woman to live."

Nell's mind had already gone back to the morning, to Tyler's warm mouth so hungry against her own, to the feel of his lean, strong body against hers. She colored at the sweet memory, and at that moment, she knew she was going to die if she could never have it again.

But Tyler didn't want her. He'd said that he didn't have room in his life for a woman—more than once. She had to keep her head. She couldn't run after him. Not when she was certain to be rejected.

"Bella, maybe I'm meant to be an old maid," she murmured thoughtfully. "Some women are, you know. It just works out that way. It's the beautiful women who marry—"

"I ain't beautiful and I married," Bella reminded her with an arrogant sniff. "Besides, looks fade. Character lasts. And you got plenty of that, child."

Nell smiled. "You're a nice lady."

"I'm glad you like me. I like me, too, just occasionally. Now wash off that spot, Nell, so we don't get food poisoning. When you have your own house and kitchen, you'll have to do all this without me to remind you."

Nell had to stifle a giggle. Bella could be imposing, but she was an angel.

Tyler threw himself into his work for the next couple of days, and Nell hardly saw him. He came to meals, but he was looking more and more haggard, and he was coughing. Since the Sunday he'd picked her up at church, they'd hardly spoken. He'd been polite but remote, and Nell began to think he was avoiding her. She understood the reason for it—he didn't want to get involved. He was probably afraid she'd read too much into those warm kisses. Well, she told herself, there was no need for him to worry. She wasn't going to throw herself at him. She just wished she could tell him so, again. But it was too embarrassing to contemplate.

All the same, she couldn't stop being concerned about him. He did look bad. Inevitably, there came a day later in the week when he didn't show up for supper.

Bella went down to the foreman's cabin to find out why. She'd asked Nell to go, but Nell had refused instantly. Another confrontation with Tyler was the last thing she needed now.

Bella came back a half hour later looking thoughtful. "He don't look too good," she remarked. "He's pale and he says he's not hungry. I hope he's not coming down with that virus that went through the bunkhouse last week."

"Is he all right?" Nell asked too quickly.

"He says a night's sleep will do him good. We'll see."

Nell watched her amble off to the kitchen and had to force herself not to go rushing down to the cabin to see Tyler. He was the epitome of good health. She knew because he'd told them that he was never sick. But there was always a first time, and he'd worked like a horse since his arrival.

Sometimes it seemed that he was working off more than the loss of his ranch back in Texas. Perhaps there'd been a girl he'd wanted who hadn't wanted him when he lost everything. That put a new perspective on things and Nell started worrying even more. She hadn't thought of him having a girlfriend. But he was a handsome man, and he was experienced. Very experienced, even to her innocent mind. There had to have been women in his past. He might even have been engaged. She groaned. She didn't like to consider the possibility that he might have kissed her because he was missing some woman he'd left behind in Texas. But it might be true. Oh, if only there was some way to find out!

She paced the living room floor until Bella complained that she was wearing out the rug. She went up to bed, where she could pace uninterrupted.

But the more she paced, the more confused things got. In the end, she undressed, put on her soft long gown and climbed into bed. Minutes later she was blessedly asleep, beyond the reach of all her problems.

The next morning, Nell's first thought was of Tyler. She dressed in jeans and a yellow knit top, looped her long hair into a ponytail, and ran downstairs with her boots barely on.

"Have you been to see Tyler?" she asked Bella.

The older woman scowled at her from a pan of biscuits she was just making up. "I will as soon as I get these biscuits in the oven...."

"I'll go."

Bella didn't say a word. But she grinned to herself as Nell went tearing out the back door.

The foreman's cabin was nice. It was big enough for a small family, but nothing fancy. Nell knocked on the door. Nobody answered. She knocked again. Still nothing.

She paused, wondering what to do. But there was really no choice. If he didn't answer, he was either asleep, which was unlikely, or gone, which was equally unlikely, or too sick to get up.

She opened the door, glad to find it unlocked, and peeked in. It was in good order for a bachelor's establishment. The Indian rugs on the floor were straight, and there were no clothes thrown over the old leather couch and chair.

Her heart beat wildly as she eased farther into the living room. "Tyler?" she called.

There was a soft groan from the bedroom. She followed it, half-afraid that she might find him totally unclothed. She looked around the door hesitantly. "Tyler?"

He was under the covers, but his hair-matted chest was bare, like his tanned, muscular arms. He opened his eyes briefly. "Nell. God, I feel rough. Can you get Bella, honey?"

"What for?" she asked gently, moving closer.

"To call a doctor," he said wearily. "I haven't slept and my chest hurts. I think I've got bronchitis." He coughed.

"I can call a doctor," she said gently. She felt his forehead. It was burning hot. "Just lie there and don't move. I'll bring you something cold to drink, and then I'll get the doctor. I'll take care of you."

He caught her eyes, searching them strangely. It felt odd, the sensation her words had sent through his body. He'd never had to be taken care of, but it occurred to him that there was nobody he'd rather have nursing him than Nell.

"Be right back," she said, hiding her concern under a faint smile. She rushed out, all the antagonism gone in the rush of concern she felt for him. He had to be all right, he just had to!

Chapter Four

Nell got Tyler a cold soft drink from his small refrigerator and helped him get a few swallows of it down before she rushed back to the main house to phone the doctor.

Bella stood listening in the doorway while Nell described the symptoms to Dr. Morrison and was told to bring Tyler in to his clinic as soon as she could get him there.

She felt insecure when she hung up. "I'll bet he thinks it could be pneumonia," Nell told the older woman worriedly. "And I guess it could be. He's coughing something terrible and burning up with fever."

"I'll go get Chappy to help you get him into the station wagon," Bella said. "Or I'll go . . ."

"No, that's all right," Nell replied. "Chappy can come with us. We'll have to postpone the daily shopping trip with the guests, but Chappy can drive the Simses and the others to the mall as soon as we get back."

"He'll hate that." Bella chuckled.

"I know, but somebody's got to look after Tyler."

Bella almost strangled herself trying to keep quiet. She could have looked after Tyler, but it was pretty obvious that Nell had already assigned that chore to herself. And Bella wasn't about to interfere. "That's right," she said, grinning. "I'll get Chappy."

But as they went out the door together, they noticed immediately that the station wagon was missing. So was the pickup truck.

"Where's he gone?" Bella yelled to Marlowe, who was leading a saddled horse out of the stable.

"Chappy had to run into town to pick up that stomach medicine for the sick calves. He's been gone a half hour, so he should be back anytime."

"Where's the pickup?" Nell called.

Marlowe shrugged. "Sorry, ma'am, I don't know."

"Great," Nell muttered. She glanced at Bella. "Well, send Chappy down to the cabin the minute he comes back. I just hope he's not inclined to linger at the vet's office."

"I'll phone the vet and make sure," Bella replied. "Don't worry. Tyler's tough."

"I guess he is." Nell sighed. She forced a smile and quickly went down the path to the cabin.

Tyler was sprawled against the pillows asleep when Nell got back to him. She sighed, wondering how on earth he was going to dress himself.

"Tyler?" she called gently, touching his bare shoulder lightly. "Tyler, wake up."

His eyes opened instantly, a little glazed from sleep and fever. "Nell?" he murmured, shifting under the covers.

"Dr. Morrison wants me to bring you to his office," she said. "We have to get you dressed."

He laughed weakly. "That's going to be harder than you think. I'm as weak as a kitten." A sudden bout of coughing doubled him up and he grimaced at the pain it caused him. "Damn! It feels like I've got a broken rib."

Nell's heart sank. It was almost surely pneumonia. Her mother had died of it, and it held hidden terrors for her because of the memory.

"Can you dress yourself?" she asked hesitantly.

He sighed jerkily. "I don't think so, Nell."

"Chappy isn't here," she said thoughtfully. "But there's Marlowe, or Bella—"

"No," he said shortly. He glared up at her with fever-bright eyes. "As strange as it may seem to you, I don't like the thought of having myself dressed by yahoos and grinning old women. No way. If you want me dressed, honey, I'll let you help. But nobody else. Not even Chappy."

That was surprising. She hadn't thought men minded people looking at them. But then, Tyler wasn't like other men.

She hesitated. "Okay. If you can get the—" she cleared her throat "—the first things on, I guess I can help with the rest."

"Haven't you seen a man without clothes?" he asked with faint humor.

"No. And I don't really want to," she said nervously.

"You may not have a choice." He started coughing again and had to catch his breath before he could speak. "Underwear and socks are in the top drawer of the dresser," he said. "Shirts and jeans in the closet."

She paused, but only for a minute. The important thing was to get him to the doctor. She had to remember that and put his health before her outraged modesty.

Since he wouldn't let anybody else help, she didn't have a choice.

As quickly as possible, she laid out everything he was going to need. But when he started trying to sit up, he held his chest and lay right back down again.

"God, that hurts, Nell," he said huskily. "It must have been the dust. We got into a cloud of it a few days ago bringing back some straying cattle, and I inhaled about half an acre, I think. I've had a lot of congestion, but I thought it was just an allergy. Until this morning, anyway."

"Oh, Tyler," she moaned.

"Should have worn my bandanna," he murmured. "That's why the old-timers wore them, you know, to pull up over their faces in dust storms and such."

"How are you going to dress?" she wailed.

He gave her a knowing look. "You mean, how are you going to dress me," he replied. "If it helps, it isn't something I'd choose to saddle you with. I don't even like stripping in front of men."

She colored. "I don't think I can," she whispered.

"It won't be that bad, I promise," he said softly. "Pull the sheet up over my hips and slide my briefs up as far as you feel comfortable. I think I can manage it from there."

The blush got worse as she picked them up. "I'm sorry," she muttered, fumbling the briefs over his feet and ankles. "Old maids aren't very good at this sort of thing."

"Neither are old bachelors." He coughed, groaning. "Come on, Nell, you can do it. Just close your eyes and push."

She laughed involuntarily. "That might be the only way." She eased them up, her hands cold against the warm, hard muscles of his thighs. She couldn't help but feel how well made he was, how powerful. She got them just under the sheet and her nerve gave way. "Is that . . . far enough?" she asked huskily.

"I'll manage." He eased his hands under the sheet and tugged and then lay back with a rough sigh. "Okay. The rest is up to you, honey."

She slid his socks on his feet. He had nice feet, very well proportioned if a little big, and even nice ankles. His legs were as tanned as his face and arms, and it almost had to be natural, because he certainly hadn't been sunbathing the past few weeks.

"This is the first time in my adult life that I've ever been dressed by a woman," he remarked weakly as she eased his undershirt over his head and pulled it down over his broad, hair-matted chest.

"They tell me there's a first time for everything," she returned, but her eyes were on the rippling muscles of his chest. She could feel the warmth of his skin, feel the thick abrasiveness of the hair that covered the broad expanse until it wedged down to his undershorts. When she reached under his arms to pull the undershirt down over his back, her face was almost pressed to his skin, and she had to grit her teeth not to kiss him there. The most unwanted sensations were washing over her body like fire. This wasn't the time or the place, she had to remind herself. He was a sick man, and she had to get him to a doctor. Besides all that, it was suicidal to feel that way about a man who'd already warned her off.

"You look like boiled lobster," he remarked. "It wasn't as bad as you thought, was it?"

"No, not really," she agreed with a thin smile. She helped him into his chambray shirt and snapped the cuffs and then the snaps down the front of it. "It's just new."

"Didn't you ever have to dress your brother?" he grinned weakly.

"No. Ted was much older than I was," she said. "And he went away to school, so we didn't spend a lot of time together. Dad and Mom worshiped him. He was their world. I guess I was more or less an accident. But they tried not to let me feel left out."

"My father never wanted kids at all," Tyler remarked. "He did his damnedest to break my spirit, and he almost did break my sister's, Shelby. But we survived. It's ironic that the ranch had to be sold. He'd have sacrificed both of us to hold on to it."

She unfolded his jeans. "You'll have your own ranch one day," she said gently. "And you won't break your children's spirits to keep it, either."

"If I have children," he replied. "Some men never marry. I may be one of them."

"Yes. I guess you might." She eased his jeans onto his long legs and pulled them up as far as she was able. They were tight and the material was thick, and it took most of her strength just to get them to his upper thighs. She knew that he'd never be able to pull them the rest of the way, not with his chest hurting so badly.

"If you can lift up, I think I can get them over your hips," she said through her teeth, and she didn't look at him as she eased the sheet away and tried not to blush at the sight of his undershorts.

"Sorry, little one," he said huskily. "But I do hurt like hell."

"I know," she said gently. "I'm not a child, after all," she said for her own benefit, as well as his. "Here goes."

She closed her eyes and pulled and tugged until she got the jeans over his hips. But she balked at the zipper, going hot all over.

"Fetch my boots, will you, honey?" he asked. He saw her hesitation and understood it. "I can manage this."

She almost wept with relief as she went to the closet to get his dress boots. She'd seen them there when she'd found his shirts and jeans. They were Tony Lama boots, exquisite and expensive, black and gleaming like wet coal.

"These are going to be hard to get on you," she said worriedly.

"You push and I'll push," he said. "They're not all that tight."

"Okay."

Between them, they worked the boots onto his feet. Then Nell got a comb and fixed his disheveled hair. And all the while he lay there against his pillow, his feverish eyes watching her, studying her in a silence that was unnerving.

The roar of a car arriving interrupted the tension. "That must be Chappy," Nell said. She caught her breath. "Tyler, you won't tell him that I . . ."

"That you helped me dress?" He smiled gently. "I won't tell anyone. It's between you and me, and no one else," he said, and the smile faded into an exchanged look that was slow and intensely disturbing. Nell's heart ran wild until she dragged her eyes away and got up to let Chappy in.

Between them, they got Tyler into the back seat of the station wagon, where he could lie down, and to Dr. Morrison's office.

The nurse helped Tyler to the examination room, while Chappy paced and Nell chewed on a fingernail. It took a long time, and she was expecting Tyler to come out with the nurse, but Dr. Morrison came to the doorway and motioned for Nell to follow him.

He beckoned her into his office, but Tyler was no-where in sight.

"He'll be fine," he told her, perching himself on the corner of his desk, "but he's got acute bronchitis."

"I was so afraid that it was pneumonia," Nell said, slumping into a chair with relief. "That pain in his chest—"

"That pain in his chest is from a pulled muscle, be-cause he's coughed so much," he said with a tolerant smile. He folded his arms across his chest. "I want him in bed until the fever goes. He can get up then, but he can't work for a full week. And then I want to see him again. I've written him two prescriptions. One's an anti-biotic, the other's an expectorant for the cough. Give him aspirin for fever and keep him in bed. If he gets worse, call me."

"Did you tell him all this?" she asked.

"Sure. He said like hell he'd lay around for a week. That's why I wanted to talk to you."

She smiled. "Thanks. He's working wonders out at the ranch. I'd hate to bury him on it."

"He seems pretty capable to me," he agreed. "Mind that he doesn't sneak out and start back to work before you realize it."

"I'll tie him in his bed," she promised.

"Bombard him with fluids while you're at it," the doctor added as he got up and opened the door. "He'll be as docile as a kitten until that antibiotic takes hold, then look out."

"I'll post guards at his door," she said with a grin. She felt lighter than air. Tyler was going to be all right. The relief was delicious. "Thank you!"

"My pleasure. He's all yours."

She smiled as she went out. If only that were true.

She called Chappy to help her get Tyler out to the station wagon, but only after she'd whispered to the receptionist to send the bill out to the ranch. She had a feeling that Tyler wouldn't appreciate having her pay his medical bill, but that was something they could argue about when he was back on his feet.

All the way home, she wondered how she was going to manage getting him undressed again. But he solved that problem himself. When they got into the cabin, he sighed and murmured, "Don't worry, Nell. I think I can manage getting out of this rig by myself."

"I'll go up to the house and get Bella to make some chicken soup for you," Nell said quickly, and darted out the door. It was easier than she'd imagined.

She sent Chappy back to town to get the prescriptions filled, because it had seemed more sensible to bring Tyler home first. She gathered the few things she might need and told Bella where she was going.

"He's not much of a threat in his present condition, I guess," Bella said, and nodded, ignoring Nell's outraged glare. "You can sleep on his sofa. But if you need me, I'm here. I can sit with him while you sleep if he gets worse in the night."

"You're a doll," Nell said.

"I have a secret Florence Nightingale streak," she corrected. "Wanted to be a nurse, once, but I faint at the sight of blood."

"They say some doctors do the first time they see an operation," Nell replied. "But I'm glad you wanted to cook, instead. You're kind of special to me."

Bella beamed, unaccustomed to the praise. "I'll have that carved on my tombstone one day. Meanwhile, you fill Tyler full of that juice I gave you and don't let him rope cattle out the window."

"I won't. Thanks, Bella."

The older woman shrugged. "I'll bring the chicken soup when it's made. I'll put some in a thermos for you."

"It'll be welcome by then. And some coffee, too, please. I don't know if Tyler has a coffeepot, but I kind of doubt it."

"He carries his around in a thermos," Bella said surprisingly. "I fill one up for him every morning and every afternoon."

"Okay. I'll get going before he escapes. See you later."

She found Tyler asleep again, apparently back in the altogether under the single sheet that covered him. Nell watched his face for a long moment, seeing the lines erased in sleep, the masculine beauty of his mouth. Just the sight of him was like a banquet to her eyes. She had to tear herself away. While he slept, she might as well make herself useful by tidying up his kitchen.

She put the juice Bella had sent in the small refrigerator, and then she washed the few dishes and cleared the counter. With that done, she checked to make sure he was still asleep before she went to the bookcase in the living room to find something to read.

Apparently he was a mystery fan, because he had plenty of books by Sir Arthur Conan Doyle and Agatha Christie on the shelves. There were some biographies and some history books about the old West, and even a book about ancient Rome. She chose a work on the Apache tribe and sat down to read it, glancing curiously at the photograph atop the bookcase. It was of a young woman with long dark hair and green eyes and a rather sad expression on her beautiful face. Beside it was a smaller photo of the same woman in white, standing beside a tall, fierce-looking man in a suit. That, she decided, had to be Tyler's sister, Shelby. Nell knew Shelby had gotten married recently, because Tyler had gone to Texas for the wedding. That man was probably her new husband. He wasn't much to look at, but perhaps he had saving graces, Nell decided.

She didn't see any other photos. That had to be a good sign. If there had been a special woman in his life, surely he'd have a picture of her. Or maybe not. If he'd lost her to someone else, he might be too bitter to keep a picture of her in a prominent place.

Feeling gloomy, she went back to the book and started reading.

Bella brought chicken soup, and Chappy brought medicine. Tyler was still asleep, but when the visitors left, Nell took his medicine, a glass of juice and a bowl of soup into the bedroom on a tray. The medicine was important, and he needed nourishment. He hadn't eaten anything all day.

She sat down gently on the bed beside him, her eyes going helplessly over his broad, bare chest and his face. "Tyler?" she said softly. He didn't stir. She reached out and hesitatingly laid one slender hand on his chest, thrilling to its hard warmth. It was the first time she'd touched a man this way, and despite the circumstances, it was blatantly pleasurable.

"Tyler, I've got your medicine," she said.

He sighed and opened his eyes slowly. "I hate medicine," he said weakly. "How about a steak?"

"Dream on. Right now, it's going to be chicken soup and encouragement. I brought you a tray."

"What time is it?"

"Almost dark," she replied. "Chappy took the guests to town to shop, and now he's holding court at the supper table. I can hear him telling tall tales through the kitchen window, and everybody's laughing."

"He tells a mean story," Tyler agreed. He breathed heavily and touched his side, encountering Nell's warm hand as his own worked its way up his chest. "You're cool," he murmured.

"Only because you have a fever," she said, thrilling to the touch of his fingers on her soft skin. "Here. Let's get some medicine into you, and then you can have soup and juice. Are you hungry?"

"Half-starved," he said. "But I don't have much appetite."

She gave him the antibiotic with a swallow of juice, and then ladled the cough syrup into his mouth.

"That tastes terrible," he muttered.

"Most medicine does," she agreed. "Can you manage to sit up while you eat?"

"Under protest." He let her prop him up with pillows and dragged himself into a sitting position. The sheet lay loosely over his hips, but she caught a glimpse of underwear, not bare skin, as he moved. "That's for your benefit," he said dryly, smiling at her color. "I drew the line at pajamas, but I wouldn't outrage your modesty too much this way."

"Thank you," she said shyly.

"Thank you," he replied. "You're stuck with me, I gather. Didn't Bella rush to play nurse?"

"She did, but I headed her off. Crowbait would have to do the cooking if she came down here, and the whole outfit would quit on the spot."

"He's not that bad," he said. "The military would love to get their hands on him. Imagine, a cook who can make a lethal weapon of an innocent biscuit."

"Shame on you," she said.

He sighed and grimaced. "I guess my biscuits aren't much better, so I don't have a lot of room to talk. Nell, I'm sorry to cave in on you like this...."

"Anybody can get sick," she said easily, and began to feed him the soup without thinking about how much feeling that simple act betrayed. "It's amazing how many people come out here from the East, thinking that their allergies will go away overnight. What they don't realize is that the dust can be as bad as pollen, and that the soil itself harbors plenty of allergens. Just listen to Mr. Davis sneeze and wheeze on trail rides, if you don't believe me."

"Well, it's the first time in my life I've had bronchitis, but I'll buck it," he said quietly. "And I'll be back at work day after tomorrow."

"No, you won't," she replied. "Dr. Morrison said you couldn't get out of bed until the fever's gone, and you can't work for a week."

He eyed her warily. "Did he tell you that?"

"He sure did," she said with a mischievous grin. "So don't try to get around me. If you do, I'll call my uncle, and then where will you be?"

"Out of work and sick, I guess," he said wearily. "Okay. I'll stay put. Under protest, you understand."

"I understand. You'll get through it. Have some more soup."

He might get through it, she thought, but would she? He slept through the night without waking, although she checked on him every hour or so until she was forced to curl up on the couch and sleep.

The next day was pretty much the same. She fed him and gave him his medicine, and he slept most of the day and all night through. But the following day he felt much better and nothing suited him. The breakfast Bella had sent over was too everything. Too hot, too much, too salty, too filling and too starchy. He didn't want to stay in bed, he had to start planning for winter, and he had to get the cattle operation in hand. That meant more work than ever, in between getting the calves ready for the fall sale. He didn't like the medicine, he hated the confinement, and Nell was beginning to wear on him, too, come to think of it.

She glared at him from red-rimmed dark eyes framed by long disheveled honey-brown hair, in the rumpled yellow knit shirt and faded jeans she'd slept in. She hadn't even bothered to put on her boots, having met Chappy at the door for the breakfast tray.

"If I wear on you, that's just too bad, Mr. Jacobs," she said shortly. "Somebody's got to keep you penned up, and everybody else is too busy. It's just the second day. The antibiotic's taking hold, and you want to fight tigers. Great. But fight them while you're asleep, please. I don't like people committing suicide on my ranch."

"It isn't your ranch yet, according to your uncle," he reminded her curtly.

"It will be," she said with cool determination. "Now you just lie down and get well."

"I don't want to lie down. I want to go to work. Hand me my clothes," he said firmly, nodding to where Chappy had draped them over his straight chair.

"Oh, no, I'm not going through that again," she said, reddening. "And you're not able to dress yourself yet—"

"Like hell I'm not able!" He pulled himself painfully into a sitting position, drew in a deep breath and tried to get his feet on the floor. He grimaced and groaned and lay back down, turning the air blue on the way down.

"Damn it, damn this disease, and damn you, too!" he swore furiously.

"Thank you. What a kind thing to say to someone who's given up regular meals and sleeping to wait on you for two days," she said icily.

"I didn't ask you to!"

"Somebody had to!" she shot back. She stuck her hands on her slender hips and glared at him. He looked all too good that way, lying back against pillows with crisp white cotton pillowcases. His chest was still bare, and his black hair hung down over his forehead, straight and thick. He looked exquisitely masculine, and the sight of his half-clothed body wasn't doing Nell's nerves any good.

"All right, thank you," he said. "You're an angel in disguise and I'll remember you in my will. Now will you get out of here and let me go back to work?"

"You can't work for a week—Dr. Morrison said so," she replied for the tenth time in as many minutes. "And he wants to see you again to make sure you're on the road to recovery. He told me not to let you on a horse."

"I don't take orders from women," he said shortly. "I work for your uncle, and I answer only to him. You don't and never have told me what to do."

"Will you listen to reason?" she demanded, passing over that bit of insolence.

"Sure. If you'll get me my pants."

"Well, I won't."

"Then I'll get them myself," he said shortly.

She folded her arms across her chest with a smile. She knew he had on his underwear, so he wasn't going to frighten her off. "Okay. Go ahead," she invited.

She didn't realize her mistake until he gave her a hard glare and abruptly threw off the sheet. Her face went from pale pink to scarlet red in seconds as he gingerly slid his long powerful bare legs over the bed and stood up. Without a stitch of clothing on.

Chapter Five

Nell was grateful that she didn't faint. What she did do was flush from the neck up and, after one long, shocked glance, turn and run out of the room.

Tyler immediately felt like a heel. He sat back down, his bad temper forgotten, and pulled the sheet over his hips. "Nell," he called gently.

She didn't answer him. She was staring out the living room window, with her arms folded tightly across her yellow shirt, trying to decide whether to stay or go. If he was going to be that difficult, she didn't know how she was going to cope. The sight of him had set her back a bit. Due to her experience with Darren McAnders when she was young, she'd led a pretty sheltered life. But she lived on a ranch, and because of that, she knew all about the technicalities of reproduction. But a nude man was a new experience. And a nude Tyler was...extraordinary. She was still shaking when she heard him calling her, more insistently.

With a deep breath, she turned and gritted her teeth and walked back to the doorway, pale and subdued.

"I'm sorry," he said tersely when he saw her face. "I won't do that again."

She shifted a little. "If you're that determined to kill yourself, I can't stop you. But for your own sake, I wish you'd do what the doctor wants."

His green eyes searched her frozen features. "I'll do damned near anything to get that look off your face. Including," he added wearily as he lay back down, "staying in the bed."

He looked tired. Probably he was, and she wished she'd been older and more sophisticated so that she wouldn't have made such a fool of herself. He made her feel about thirteen.

"Can I get you anything?" she asked.

"I could do with some more juice," he said. "And if you'll dig me out some fresh underwear, I'll put it back on again."

She felt hot all over and tried to hide her reaction to him as she got him a glass of juice and then took a pair of briefs from the dresser. As she put them beside him, he caught her wrist and pulled her down onto the bed, holding her there firmly while he looked at her.

"How can you be twenty-four years old and so damned innocent?" he asked quietly. "Especially with all the people who pass through here in a year's time?"

"I don't mix with people very much," she said. Her eyes slid helplessly over his broad, bare chest. "I socialize only to the extent that I have to, and since most people who come here keep to themselves except for organized activities, I don't have many problems. If I had my own way, this would be just a cattle ranch and I wouldn't take in paying guests. But the dude ranch part is paying for the cattle operation, so I don't have much choice.''

"Do you date?''

She kept her eyes down. "No, I don't have time.''

"So many secrets between us, Nell,'' he said, caressing her hand lightly. "Too many.''

"You told me you weren't interested in involvement. Well, I'm not either,'' she lied.

"Really? Or is it that you don't think you attract men?''

She remembered when she'd said that and what he'd done about it on the way home from church. Her lips parted as she remembered the hungry kiss they'd shared, and she had to fight not to throw herself down against him and beg him to do it again.

"I can't attract men,'' she replied tersely.

"You're a pretty woman,'' he said. "You downplay your attractions, but they're there. Why don't you buy a new dress, have your hair done and put on some make-up for the next Saturday square dance?'' he murmured, reaching up to tug on a long lock of her hair. "And I'll teach you to dance.''

Breathing grew harder by the minute. She felt nervous and insecure, and the slow tracing of his long fingers on her hand and wrist was beginning to stir her blood.

"It's not practical,'' she said inanely, because she could hardly think at all.

"Why not?''

"Because...because you're...'' She bit her lip. "You're just bored, Tyler, and when you're back on your feet again, when you're working for yourself again... Oh, I'm just muddling it.''

"You think I'm playing.''

She sighed. "Yes.''

He took her hand and pulled it to his chest, pressing it hard over the hair-covered expanse where his heart was beating like a bass drum. "Nell, am I callous enough to play with a virgin?" he asked softly.

Of course he wasn't, but she couldn't keep her thoughts clear. The effect he had on her was incredible, and she was hungry for an affection she'd never had from a man.

"It doesn't matter," he said huskily, pulling on her hand. "Come here."

"Tyler, you're sick—"

"I don't have any fever, and I feel like a new man." He eased her across him until she was on her back in the bed with his lean bare torso above her, his green eyes glittering down at her. "I've never seen a woman with less self-confidence than you have, Nell," he said. "There's nothing wrong with the way you look or the way you are."

"Tyler, you're scaring me," she whispered. Her hands went to his chest, and part of her tried to protest. This was bringing back terrible memories of another man she'd loved, or thought she loved, and his harsh, hurtful treatment of her. But Tyler wasn't McAnders, and the look on his face was intoxicating. He wanted her. Not as a substitute for another woman, but for herself.

"No, that won't work," he said gently. His lean hands cupped her chin and held her face tilted up to his. "I'm not going to be rough with you, not ever. And anything we do together will be because you want it."

That was as new as her proximity to him, and she began to relax. There was nothing threatening about him. He seemed fully in control and lazily indulgent.

"Yes, that's it," he said as he felt the tension draining out of her body. "I'm not going to hurt you."

As he spoke, his dark head bent. She felt his mouth whispering over her eyelids, closing them, brushing her nose, her chin, and then settling softly over her mouth. Her breath seemed suspended while he found just the right pressure, the right mingling of tenderness and expertise to make her lips part for him. And while he kissed her, his lean hands slid under her blouse at the back, and she thrilled to the faint roughness of their touch on her bare skin.

He was addictive, she thought dizzily, enraptured by the warmth of his caresses. She didn't think she could have pulled away to save her life. Every touch was more exciting than the one before. His mouth became a necessity. Without its warm crush she was sure to die.

Shyly, she flattened her hands against his chest and let them experience the thickness of hair, the strong padding of muscle beneath it. His breath caught against her mouth, and her eyes opened, questioning.

"I'm sorry, I didn't mean to..." she began quickly.

"It feels good," he said, smiling down into her shocked face. "I can drag that sound out of you the same way."

Her body coiled inside, like a kitten anticipating being stroked. She felt herself tremble and wondered at the mental pictures that were flashing sensually through her mind. His hands on her, touching her...there. Her lips parted. "You...you can?" she whispered, which wasn't what she wanted to say at all, but she was too shy and inexperienced to put it into words.

Tyler, with his greater experience, knew immediately that she was going to welcome whatever he wanted to do. It went to his head, making his thoughts spin with new possibilities. His hands had already told him that Nell had been hiding her light, physically at least, under a barrel. He needed the intimacy with her as he'd needed nothing else in his life, although he still didn't quite understand the way she affected his senses.

"Yes," he breathed, bending again to her mouth. "I can."

As his lips toyed with hers, his hand went to the fastening of her bra. Subtly, almost without her knowing it, he released the catch and slid his fingers slowly, exploringly, under her arm to the soft edge of her breast.

She trembled, but she didn't pull away or protest, and his blood ran hot and fast through his veins. He wanted to look at her. He wanted to see her eyes when he touched her.

He lifted his head. The glitter of his eyes unnerved her at first, until she felt again the light tracing of his fingers against her skin. The sensations piled on each other until she went hot all over with the need to make him put his hand on her, to touch her. Her body was more demanding than her mind, because it tried to twist toward him, to force a contact he was deliberately denying her.

"Ty...ler?" she whispered brokenly.

His free hand was under her nape. It moved caressingly in her thick hair while his gaze searched her huge, hungry eyes. "Shhhhh," he whispered gently. The hand under her arm moved again, tracing, and she arched, shuddering, while her big eyes pleaded with him. "It's all right," he whispered. "It's all right, honey."

And all the while, his fingers were driving her mad. She felt as if every single cell in her body was drawn as tight as a rope, as if the tension was going to break her in half. Her nails contracted on his muscular upper arms and dug in, and when she realized it, she was shocked at her own action.

"I'm...sorry," she whispered jerkily, caressing the red crescents she'd made in his skin. "I'm sorry, I...couldn't...help it."

"You haven't hurt me," he said gently. "You know that I'm doing this deliberately. Do you know why?"

"No," she whimpered, jerking as his fingertips edged a little farther onto her breast.

"It's very much like a symphony, little one," he whispered softly, and he managed a smile. "It starts slowly, softly, and builds and builds and builds to a crescendo. When I finally give you what you're pleading for, Nell, you're going to feel a kind of pleasure that I can't even describe to you."

Her teeth ground together, because the tension was growing unbearable. "But...when...?"

"Now." His mouth covered hers and his hand moved, at last, at last, at...last! It covered her breast, swallowing up the hard tip, giving her the tiny consummation her body had begged for.

And it was like fireworks. She cried out into his mouth, shuddered, arched with the anguished fulfillment. Her hand found his through the cloth of her shirt and pressed against it, holding it prisoner. She sobbed, and the hand at her neck contracted as his mouth grew feverishly hungry. For long, fiery seconds, the sounds of their breathing were audible in the quiet room.

"It isn't enough," he bit off against her mouth. While he held her, his hand began to unbutton her shirt. He lifted his head and looked into her eyes. "I won't go farther than this, I promise you," he said huskily. "But I...need...to look at you."

Her eyelids felt heavy. She couldn't work up the effort to protest. What he'd just given her was like honey, and she was helpless with pleasure. She wanted more. She wanted his eyes on her.

It was extraordinary, she thought, watching him divest her of her shirt and bra. Extraordinary, that look in his eyes, on his face, as he eased her down against the pillows and sat gazing at her taut, swollen breasts.

"Ty," she whispered. "There was a movie I watched once, and it was just a little racy. But the man . . . he did more than touch her. He put his mouth . . ."

"Here?" he whispered back, brushing her taut breast with the backs of his fingers, his eyes intent on hers.

She jerked involuntarily with pleasure. "Yes."

"Do you want that, with me?"

She colored, but she was beyond pretending. "Oh, yes . . . !"

His mouth eased down over the soft flesh, smoothing her skin, sensitizing it. The sensation was beyond anything she'd ever imagined. She made little whimpers that sent his mind whirling out of control. He groaned against her breast and gathered her up close, giving in to the need to taste her, to pleasure her.

She didn't hear the knock the first time it came. But the second time it was louder. She lay still, listening, and felt Tyler stiffen above her.

He caught his breath slowly, glancing through the open bedroom door toward the living room with glazed eyes and a mind that was still in limbo.

"Mr. Jacobs, I brought your mail. I'll slide it under the door."

It was Chappy's voice, and thank God he went away quickly. Nell colored furiously as she imagined what would have happened if Chappy had just walked in.

Tyler looked down at her quietly, letting his bold gaze go from her eyes to her swollen mouth to the alabaster skin of her breast.

"Are you all right?" he whispered softly. "I didn't frighten you?"

"No." She was looking at him as intently as he was studying her, measuring memory and imagination against the sweet reality of what they'd done together. "Not at all."

He touched her breast tenderly and smiled at her. "It was good," he whispered.

"Yes."

He eased down on his elbows and slowly drew his chest over her sensitized breasts, watching her shiver and gasp with the delicious sensation of it. "This is good, too," he breathed, bending again to her mouth. "I want you, Nell."

She tensed as his mouth brushed hers, and he smiled against her trembling lips.

"I'm not going to do anything about it," he reassured her. "Kiss me, and then you'd better get out of here."

She slid her arms up around his neck and gave him her mouth in a kiss as sweet and wild as the ones before. But seconds later he drew away and rolled over, taking her with him. He lay on his back, shuddering a little with a need he couldn't fulfill.

"You might as well get rid of the baggy britches and loose blouses," he murmured, holding her bare breasts against his broad chest. "I'll never fall for the camouflage again, after this."

"Am I too big?" she whispered, because it mattered if she was.

He brushed the hair away from her mouth. "No. You're just right. All of you." He brushed a warm kiss against her lips and loosened his arms. "You'd better get your things back on. I'm weak, but I'm still capable. I don't want this to get out of hand."

She touched his face, her fingers cold and nervous, tracing its hard contours, fascinated with him. "You can't imagine what it was like for me," she whispered. "I... well, it wasn't what I thought it would be."

He smiled. "Not even after you saw that racy movie?" he murmured dryly.

She swallowed, remembering when she'd told him about it and what had followed. "Well, no. Seeing and experiencing are different."

"Indeed they are." He helped her to sit up and spent a long minute looking at her before he gathered up her bra and blouse and proceeded to help her back into them. "No," he said when she tried to stop him. "You dressed me. Now it's my turn."

So she sat still and let him dress her, delighting in his gentle touch, in his obvious pleasure in her.

"You can't stay here tonight," he said. "I hope you realize why."

"Yes. I know why."

He buttoned her up to the throat and smoothed back her long disheveled hair. "I would like very much to take your clothes off and pull you under this sheet with me and love you up to the ceiling," he said seriously. "I could do that, despite your innocence. But I'd hate myself for abusing your trust, and you might hate me for backing you into a corner. I don't want anything to spoil what's building between us. I don't think you want that, either."

She linked her fingers into his as he toyed with her hair. "No. I don't want anything to spoil it, either," she whispered.

He drew her hand to his mouth and kissed it gently. "I won't sleep. I'll remember how it was while we were loving each other in this bed, and I'll ache to have you here with me."

She trembled at his description of what they'd done. It had felt like loving, even if he only meant that in a physical sense. Her warm eyes searched his, and her face was radiant with shared pleasure, with hope, with new dreams that seemed to be turning into reality.

"I never dreamed it would be this way," she said absently.

"How did you think it would be?"

"Frightening," she confessed without telling him why. McAnders had made it into a terrifying thing, a violent act that would have hurt if he'd succeeded. But what she'd experienced with Tyler wasn't terrifying. It had been beautiful.

"And it wasn't?" he persisted gently.

"Not frightening, no," she said with a demure smile. "A little scary, but in a nice way. So many sensations..."

"For me, too, Nell," he said somberly. His eyes held hers. "That was no casual diversion, and don't you forget it. I'm not a playboy."

"You're not a monk, either," she said. She smiled shakily. "I may be innocent, but I'm not stupid."

He sighed, smoothing her closed fingers with his thumb. "If you want the truth, yes, I've had women. But always women who couldn't or wouldn't consider marriage or anything permanent. And never for money. Lovemaking is too beautiful to reduce to a quick coupling that only satisfies a casual hunger."

She couldn't speak. She hadn't expected him to say anything like that, and it occurred to her that she didn't really know him very well. "I'm glad you think of it that way," she said.

"Don't you, honestly?" he asked.

"With you I do," she said after a minute. McAnders's angry handling was fading away like a bad dream. Now when she thought about physical expressions of affection, she was always going to feel Tyler's hands on her body.

He touched her lips with a long forefinger. "Go away," he said softly. "I want you terribly, Miss Regan."

She smiled tenderly. "I'm very glad of that. But I'll go."

She got up from the bed, her eyes possessive as they ran over his taut body.

"Would you like an anatomy lesson?" he asked with a dry smile. "I could pull this sheet away and teach you volumes about men."

She averted her eyes, her cheeks scarlet. "I'll just bet you could," she muttered, because she remembered how his body had changed when hers came into contact with it. "And stop making fun of me because I'm not clued in."

"I happen to like you that way, believe it or not," he mused. "Come back in the morning. We can have another argument."

"I don't really want to argue with you."

"The alternative could get us into real trouble."

She laughed because he sounded so morose and dryly amused all at once. Her face changed with the sound, brightened, went soft and radiant.

"You are lovely when you laugh," he said huskily. "And if you don't get out of here right now, I'm going to throw off this damned sheet and come after you."

She let out a low whistle and headed for the door. "The mind boggles," she murmured as she glanced over her shoulder and smiled at him. "Sleep tight."

"Oh, that's funny," he agreed. "A real screamer. I'll have to remember to put it in my memoirs."

"I won't sleep, either," she said softly, and left him reluctantly.

She went out the door smiling, her heart so light that it could have floated before her. She'd never been so happy in all her life. The most unexpected things happened sometimes. They'd argued and she'd been sure that there was no hope, and now he'd kissed her so hungrily, handled her so gently that she was building daydreams again. This had to be the real thing, she told herself doggedly. He'd told her he wasn't playing, so it had to be for real. It had to be!

And all of a sudden, she started thinking about the past, about a man who'd teased her and kissed her lazily once or twice, a man she'd thought she loved. And that man had betrayed her trust and tried to force her into bed, all because he'd wanted her bright, beautiful sister-in-law. It didn't bear thinking about. Surely history wasn't going to repeat itself with Tyler. Nell closed her eyes in faint fear. She couldn't bear the thought of that.

If Bella noticed that Nell's lips were swollen and her hair wildly disheveled and her face full of a new radiance mingled with fear, she kept it to herself. But she was less abrasive than usual as Nell helped with the dishes, and she was smiling when the younger woman went up to bed.

Nell awoke the next morning after a sleepless night to hear a furious commotion going on down in the kitchen.

She hurriedly dressed in jeans and a neat checked shirt, left her hair down around her shoulders and went to the kitchen for breakfast. She caught the tail end of a conversation that sounded curious at best.

Bella was still raging at someone. "...can't imagine what possessed him! Of course he didn't know—he isn't a mean kind of man. But we've got to get him out of here!"

"Can't be done." That was Chappy's voice, slow and measured. "Old Man Regan gave him the power to hire and fire. Even Nell can't override him in something like this. It's just a damned shame that one of you women didn't think to tell him!"

"Well, it ain't the kind of thing you talk about to outsiders," Bella grumbled.

"He was up and moving about last I looked. Should I go talk to him?"

"Hold off a few minutes. Give me time to think."

"Okay. Tell me when."

A door slammed. Nell hesitated before she went on into the room. When Bella saw her, she turned beet red.

"Nell! I wasn't expecting you this early," she said with a toothy grin that was as false as fool's gold.

"I heard you," Nell said. "What's going on? Is it something to do with the new men? They're supposed to show up today." She gnawed her lower lip. "I guess we can send them on over to Tyler. He was much better yesterday. He can't work, but he can still delegate—"

"You'd better sit down," Bella began.

"Why? Has he hired Jack the Ripper?" Nell grinned. She felt great. It was a beautiful day, and she wanted to get this over with so that she could see Tyler. Her whole life had changed overnight. Everything was beautiful.

"Worse." Bella took a deep breath. "Oh, there's just no use in pussyfooting around. He's hired Darren McAnders."

There was a hush like death in the room. Of all the things Nell might have expected to hear, that was the last. She did sit down, heavily, with her heart in her throat. Nightmares were rushing in on her, old wounds were opening.

"How could he?" she asked huskily. "How could he give that man a job here? I thought Darren was working on a ranch in Wyoming."

"Obviously he came home, and it seems he thought nine years had healed old wounds."

"Not mine," Nell said, her dark eyes flashing. "Not ever. He used me. He hurt me, scared me out of my mind... Well, he isn't going to work here. Tell Chappy to fire him."

"You know Chappy can't do that. Neither can you," Bella said. "You'll have to go and tell Tyler what happened."

She went white. After what she and Tyler had shared the day before, the thought of telling him about what McAnders had done to her was sickening. Not only that, she'd have to tell him all of it. That McAnders had flirted with her and teased her, just as Tyler had done. That he'd made a little light love to her, and she'd gone off the deep end and thrown herself at him. It had never been all Darren's fault—even in the beginning. Nell hadn't been able to talk to Bella or Margie, to tell them how much at fault *she'd* been. But she'd loved Darren, or thought she had, and she'd assumed from his affectionate advances that he felt the same way. She'd had the shock of her young life when he'd come into her room, expecting her cooperation to help get Margie out of his blood, and found her unwilling and apparently scared to death. He'd had some harsh things to say, and he'd been drinking. She still didn't know if he'd have gone far enough to force her, because her screams had brought Bella and Margie running. Surely Darren didn't think Nell was still carrying a torch for him and would welcome him back? He had to know how she hated him.

"Tell Tyler what happened," Bella said. "He'll understand."

Nell wasn't at all sure that he would. She thought of approaching Darren, but she couldn't bear to talk to him. Nine years hadn't erased her shame and fear of him, or her embarrassment for her own behavior that had led to such a tragic confrontation.

"I'll try," Nell promised as she went out the back door. She wasn't going to confess, she knew that. But maybe there was another way.

She knocked on Tyler's door, shaking in her boots. He called for her to come in, and she found him in the kitchen, frying eggs.

He glanced at her with a strange reserve, as if he'd forgotten the day before or didn't want to remember it. "Good morning," he said quietly. His eyes slid over her and quickly away, back to what he was doing. "Do you want some breakfast?"

His coolness robbed her of courage. He didn't seem like the same man who'd kissed her half to death. Perhaps he was ashamed. Perhaps he regretted every kiss. Or perhaps he was just afraid she might throw herself at him. Shades of the past fell ominously over her head.

"I'm not hungry." She took a deep breath. "One of the new men you hired is Darren McAnders. I want you to let him go. Right now."

His black eyebrows arched. He moved the pan from the burner and shut off the stove before he turned slowly to face her. "I don't think I heard you right."

"I said I want you to fire McAnders right now," she returned stiffly. "I won't have him on this ranch."

"How many available cowboys do you think I can find at roundup time?" he asked shortly. "I'm already a man short, even with McAnders, and he comes highly recommended by the Wyoming outfit he was working for. He's steady, he doesn't drink, and he knows what to do with a rope. And you want me to fire him before he's even started? You little fool, he could sue us to hell for that and bring down half the government on our heads!"

"You won't do it?" she asked coldly.

"No." He glowered at her. "Not without cause. If you want him fired, tell me why," he said, and his eyes were oddly intent.

She tried. She started to speak. Her sweet memories were turning black in her mind, and she was already mourning for what might have been. Tyler looked formidable. He also looked fighting mad. She'd gone about it all wrong. She should have tried honey instead of vinegar, but it was too late now. He'd see right through that tactic, anyway.

"We're old enemies," she said finally. "That's the best I can do by way of an explanation."

He smiled mockingly and there was a new coldness in his tone. "Now that's interesting," he said. "Because McAnders told me this morning that you were old friends. Very close friends, in fact."

Chapter Six

Nell just stood, staring blankly at Tyler while she tried to decide what to say. His tone was enough to convince her that he was well on the way to believing that she'd lied to him. God knew what Darren had said about the past, but it had made a terrible difference in Tyler's attitude toward her. She could feel the distrust in him, and it chilled her.

"You don't have to agonize over an explanation," Tyler said when he saw her hesitation. It was obvious that McAnders had meant something to her. "But don't expect me to fire a man because he's one of your old flames," he added mockingly. "That isn't reason enough."

She didn't say another word. He was looking at her as if he was prepared to disbelieve anything she said. He didn't know her well enough to see that she'd never have asked him to fire a man out of some personal grudge. It went much deeper than that. McAnders was an unpleasant part of her past, a constant reminder of her own lack of self-control, her vulnerability. Tyler had shown her that physical desire wasn't the terrible thing she'd remembered. But that was over before it began, all because she couldn't bring herself to tell him the truth.

"Nothing else to say?" he asked.

She shook her head. "No, thank you. I'm sorry I disturbed you."

Tyler scowled as she left. She was subdued now when she'd been fiery-tempered before. What was McAnders to her? Was she still in love with him and afraid of succumbing? Or was it something more? He wished he'd made her tell him. Now, he had a terrible feeling that he might have left it too late.

Nell was keyed up and frightened of her first confrontation with Darren. It came unexpectedly that same day, at dusk, when he was passing the back porch as she went out the door.

She looked up and there he was. Her first love. Her first crush. Until Tyler had come along, her only crush. Darren McAnders had been in his early twenties nine years ago. Now he was in his early thirties, but he hadn't changed. He had dark auburn hair, threaded with gray at the temples now, and blue eyes. He was a little heavier than he had been. But it was his face that drew Nell's attention the most. He'd aged twenty years. He had lines where he shouldn't have had them, and the easygoing smile she remembered was gone completely.

"Hello, Nell," he said quietly.

She didn't flinch, although she felt like it. He brought back memories of her own stupidity and its near-disastrous consequences. He was walking proof that her self-control was a myth, and she didn't like it.

"Hello, Darren," she replied.

"I suppose you've given the word to have me thrown off the place by now," he said surprisingly. "Once I knew you still lived here, I was sure I'd made a mistake in hiring on without telling your new ramrod the truth." He frowned slightly, pushing his battered hat back on his head. "You don't mind that I'm here?"

"Of course I mind," she said coldly, and her dark eyes flashed. "I mind that I made a fool of myself over you, and that you used me because of Margie. But if you don't mind the memories, then neither do I. Keep your job. I don't care one way or the other."

He searched her face for a long moment, and then what he could see of her body in her usual clothing, and a kind of sadness claimed his expression. "You might not believe it, but I had a lot of regrets about what happened. It's been heavy on my conscience all these years."

He looked as if it had, too, and that was the most surprising thing of all to Nell. She didn't speak because she couldn't think of anything to say.

He took a slow breath. "How is Marguerite?" he asked finally.

She'd suspected that Marguerite's widowhood had some place in McAnders's decision to take a job at the ranch. Even nine years hadn't dimmed his passion for Margie. Nell wondered how Margie would react.

"She's doing very well," Nell replied. "She and her sons live in Tucson. They come out here for an occasional weekend."

"I heard about your brother," he remarked. "I'm sorry. I always liked Ted. I hated betraying his trust that way."

"He never knew how you felt about her," she said. "Now if you'll excuse me..."

"You've changed," he said suddenly. "I wouldn't have known you in that getup."

She flushed with mingled temper and embarrassment as she remembered the close-fitting outfits she used to wear to try to catch his eye. "I guess not," she said tightly. "We all change with age."

"Not as much as you have." He grimaced. "Oh, Nell," he said softly. "Ted should have shot me for what I did to you. He should have shot me dead."

And he turned on his heel and walked away before she could reply. That wasn't the Darren McAnders she remembered. He was no longer the cocky, arrogant young man who'd alternately teased and toyed with her. He was older and far more mature, and the teasing streak seemed to have been buried. All the same, it was too soon to start trusting him, and Margie was going to have a fit when she heard that he was back on the ranch.

Bella had the same feeling, because after supper was cleared away she mentioned that it might be a good idea for Nell to call and tell Margie about their new hand.

"I won't," Nell said firmly. "She'll find out soon enough. She and the boys are coming this weekend."

Bella sighed. "Going to be fireworks," she said.

"Then she can complain to Tyler. I didn't hire him."

"Nell!"

She jumped. Tyler's deep voice carried even when he didn't raise it, but it was clearly raised now, and irritated as he came down the hall toward the kitchen.

"Is that you, or did somebody stick a pin in a mountain lion?" Nell asked with more courage than she felt.

He didn't smile. He was bareheaded and grim, and there were several bills held in one lean hand. "We've got to talk," he said.

Nell glanced apprehensively at Bella, but the older woman began to whistle as if she hadn't heard a word. Nell put down the dishcloth and followed Tyler back down the hall to the front room that served as an office.

The desk was cluttered, and it looked as if Tyler had been at the books for at least a couple of hours. He'd been going over the ranch's finances for several weeks now, in his spare time, trying to make sense of Nell's hit-or-miss bookkeeping system. Apparently he'd just figured it out, and he didn't like what he saw.

"These—" he indicated a new set of books "—are the new books. I've boiled everything down to credits and debits. From now on, every purchase comes through me. If you want a needle and thread, you'll have to have a purchase order. This—" he held up a book of purchase orders "—is a book of them. It's going to be locked in the desk, and I have the only key."

"Why?" she asked.

He motioned her into a chair and perched himself on the corner of the desk to light a cigarette. "The way things have been run here, any cowboy could go to the hardware store and charge butane or vaccination supplies or go to the feed store for feed or salt and charge it without any authorization." He handed her the bills he'd been carrying. "Read a couple of those."

She frowned curiously, but she did as she was told. "A pair of spurs," she murmured, reading aloud, "a new saddle..." She looked up. "I never authorized those."

"I know you didn't." He smiled faintly. "That's the problem with giving carte blanche to the cowboys."

"Who had the saddle and spurs on here?" she demanded.

"Marlowe."

"You ought to fire him."

"I already have," he said. "Good thing I hired on two new men instead of one." He eyed the tip of his cigarette. "I saw you talking to McAnders. Is there still a problem?"

She didn't feel comfortable discussing it with him. "There won't be one. Darren and I will work things out."

That sounded ominous to him. As if she had ideas about recapturing the past. He scowled at her, his green eyes almost sparking with bad temper. "As long as you keep your dalliance after working hours, I don't care what you do."

She felt something inside her dying. He couldn't know how badly he was hurting her with his indifference. She supposed he wouldn't care if he did. She lowered her eyes to her jeans. "Have you told the men about the purchase orders?"

"I told the crew in the bunkhouse at supper. I'll tell the married hands in the morning. There are going to have to be other changes, as well." He picked up the ledger and went through it. "For one thing, we're going to have to cut back on the activities that require cowboy participation. It's getting time for roundup, and I'll need every man I've got. This open range may be fine for a big outfit, but it's hell on one this size. We'll spend the better part of a week just getting the saler calves into holding pens."

"We can borrow Bob Wyler's helicopter, if you want to," Nell said. "He always helps out that way, and he supplies the pilot, too."

"For what kind of payment?" Tyler asked narrowly.

Nell grinned involuntarily. "For a case of Bella's strawberry-rhubarb preserves," she said.

He chuckled, too, in spite of himself. "Okay. That's a deal. But can you manage the trail rides without Chappy?"

"I managed well enough before Ted died," she said. "I can do it again. What else?"

"This is the worst of it. We're spending a fortune on having a golf pro on the payroll for visitors who want to tee off on the Western Terrace greens. That's fine for the big dude ranches, but we're operating on a shoestring here. I can show you on paper that only one out of every ten guests avails himself of this service, but the pro collects his fee just the same."

"That was Ted's idea," she said. "I've just let it drag on. You may have noticed that most of the people who come here aren't really very athletic." She blushed and he laughed.

"Yes, I've noticed." He searched her dark eyes slowly, and little sparks of attraction seemed to leap between them before he drew his gaze down to his cigarette. "Then I'll take care of the pro. As for this daily shopping trip into Tucson, is that mandatory?"

"We could cut back to every other day," she compromised. "I realize that it's pretty hard on the gas budget, what with the van being used for transportation. I guess the city tour is hard on the budget, too."

He nodded his dark head. "That was going to be my next question. Can we subcontract the tours out to an existing agency in town?"

"Sure! I know a terrific lady who'd love the business, and her fees are very reasonable."

"Okay. Give her a call and work something out."

"You've been working," Nell remarked, nodding toward all the ledgers and paperwork.

"It's been a long job. But I didn't want to make specific recommendations until I had a handle on how the ranch was run. You haven't done a bad job, Nell," he said surprisingly. "Except for a few places, you've budgeted to the bone. You've only continued old policies. But we're going to change some of those and get this place operating in the black again."

"You sound encouraging."

"It's a good little operation," he replied. "It shouldn't be hard to make it a paying one. Anyplace you think you may need more help?"

She thought for a minute, trying not to notice the way his jeans clung to his long, powerful legs, or the fact that the top three buttons of his red-checked shirt were unbuttoned over that tanned expanse of hair-covered chest. She remembered all too well how it had felt to touch him in passion.

"I'd like to have someone come with me on the trail ride while that man from back East is here," she confessed with a faint smile. "His wife is rather cold-eyed, and she seems to have some insane idea that I'm chasing him."

Tyler's eyes went narrow. "Yes, I saw how he tried to come on to you at the square dance. They leave Thursday, don't they?" He saw her nod. "I'll go on the next two trail rides with you. Chappy can keep things in order for Bella while we're out."

"Thanks."

"Unless you'd rather I let McAnders go with you?" he added with a mocking smile.

She wanted to protest, but that would be a little too revealing. She swallowed. "Whatever suits you," she said. "It doesn't matter to me."

Which wasn't the answer he wanted. He put out his cigarette with faint violence. "McAnders can go with you, then," he said. "I've got enough work to do without playing nursemaid."

The words were meant to sting, and they did. She got up, avoiding his eyes as she went to the door. "Thanks for all you're doing," she said over her shoulder.

"My pleasure. Good night."

"Good night."

She didn't see him alone after that. There was always some reason to have other people present or to put off discussions until she could arrange for reinforcements. But that didn't stop Tyler from cutting at her verbally at every opportunity.

What hurt the most was that Darren McAnders didn't mind accompanying her on trail rides, and seemed even to enjoy her taciturn company. He began to smile again, as if being with her brightened his life. She didn't understand why, and she understood even less Tyler's new antagonism.

But the fire hit the fan on the weekend, when Margie and the boys arrived by taxi.

Nell had just come back from the trail ride, with Darren McAnders at her side. Marguerite, immaculate in a white linen suit, stepped out of the cab she'd recklessly hired in Tucson, with her long reddish-gold hair wafting in the breeze, and looked straight up into Darren McAnders's stunned face.

"Darren!" she exclaimed, missing her step.

She went down on her knees in the dust, and Darren vaulted out of the saddle to pick her up, his hands strong and sure on her upper arms, his eyes intent on her flushed face.

"Margie," he said softly. "You haven't aged. You're as beautiful as ever."

"What are you doing here?" Margie gasped. She glanced at Nell, even more shocked to find Nell apparently voluntarily in Darren's company.

"He's our newest hand," Nell told her. "Tyler hired him."

"Doesn't he know?" Margie asked, and then flushed when she saw Darren's rueful smile. "Oh, I'm sorry. It's just that..."

"The past is only a problem if we let it be," Nell said stubbornly. "Darren and I are getting along very well. Aren't we, Darren?" she asked.

He smiled ruefully. "As well as could be expected. Nell's been very generous. It was this job or welfare, and I couldn't have blamed her if she'd thrown me off the place. It's as much as I deserved."

Margie searched his face slowly and then glanced up at Nell, sitting still on her horse. "It took a lot of courage for you to come back here, Darren," she remarked, even though she was looking at Nell, waiting, questioning.

"I found out that running away doesn't solve much," he said enigmatically. He glanced past Margie. "Are these your boys?" He asked the question softly, and his eyes echoed that softness as he looked at them. "Curt and Jess, aren't you? Your Aunt Nell's said a lot about you."

They piled out of the car like marauding pirates and stared at him enthusiastically. "Did she, really?" Curt asked. "Did she say nice stuff? Me and Jess are lots of help around the ranch—Tyler says so. We help him find snakes and lizards and stuff and keep them from eating up Aunt Nell's cattle!"

Aunt Nell's eyes widened with amusement. "Did Tyler tell you that?"

"Well, not really," Jess murmured. "But it sounds good, don't it?"

"Doesn't it," Margie corrected absently. She was just beginning to get her self-confidence back after the shock of seeing Darren. "Boys, we'd better get inside." She paid the driver, and Nell got off her horse to help with the luggage, but Darren was one step ahead of her.

"I'll take care of this if you can manage the horses, Nell," he said with a hopeful glance in her direction.

She knew he'd never gotten over Margie. It didn't surprise her that he was anxious to renew that acquaintance. What Margie felt was less easy to perceive. But it certainly wasn't like the older woman to lose her step and pitch headfirst into desert sand.

"Sure," Nell agreed easily. "I'll take them to the barn. Margie, I'll see you and the boys in a few minutes."

"That's fine," Margie said absently, but she was looking at Darren as if she'd been poleaxed.

Nell was faintly relieved. With Darren around, maybe Margie wouldn't bat her eyelashes so luxuriously at Tyler. Not that it mattered anymore. Tyler had certainly made it clear that he wasn't interested in Nell. He avoided her like the very plague.

She led the horses to the barn, where Chappy took the reins with a curious glance at her rigid features.

"You okay?" he asked.

She smiled. "I'm fine." She glanced around. "Where's Caleb?"

Caleb was the big black gelding that Tyler always rode. Asking for the horse's whereabouts was a little less obvious than inquiring about Tyler's.

Chappy saw right through her. "He's out riding the boundary fence we put up around the holding pens."

She blinked. "He hates riding fence."

"He overheard two of the boys talking about the way McAnders hangs around you since he's been here," the wrinkled cowboy said with a twinkle in his pale blue eyes. "He set them to cleaning out the stables, and he went off to ride fence. I don't reckon anybody will mention such things around him again, once word gets through the outfit."

She bit her lower lip. "Why should he care?"

Chappy started to lead the horses toward the stable, where two sweating, swearing cowboys were mucking out the stalls and pitching fresh hay. "You need glasses," he said dryly.

Nell drifted back to the house slowly, her eyes everywhere on the horizon, looking for a glimpse of Tyler. Things had been strained between them. That, and McAnders's presence, were making her life miserable. Not that she minded Darren being around. He'd changed so much from the shallow, careless man she'd known. She felt no remnant of the old crush she'd had on him, nor any sense of bitterness. He was like a friendly stranger whom she began to like, but nothing more.

If only she could go to Tyler and tell him that. But despite his odd behavior this afternoon, he hadn't said anything that would lead Nell to believe he had any lasting affection for her. In fact, he'd said more than once that there wasn't any place for a woman in his life right now. And the thought of throwing herself at another man, after the misery her encounter with Darren had brought her, was unwelcome. Tyler might be kind about it, but she knew he wouldn't appreciate having her "hang on his boots," as he'd mentioned to Bella.

She sighed. She knew so little about men. If only she could talk to Margie, perhaps she could find a way out of the corner she'd painted herself into.

She went into the house to help Bella get supper on the table before the guests were called onto the elegant patio to eat. The wooden tables each had umbrellas and sat beside an Olympic-size swimming pool, which did a lot of business during the day. All meals were taken here, with Bella and Nell setting a buffet table from which guests could choose their portions. All around were palo verde trees, along with every conceivable form of cactus known to the desert Southwest. It was amusing to watch the guests from back East ask about the flower garden mentioned in the brochure and then see it for real. The native plants were surrounded by rock borders, and their arrangement was both mysterious and compelling. In bloom, the cacti were beautiful, like the feathery palo verde with its fragrant yellow blossoms.

"You aren't eating?" Nell asked when Margie sat down a good distance away from the guests while, as a special treat, the boys had their meal in the bunkhouse with the cowboys.

Margie shook her head. She'd changed into designer jeans and a red tank top, and she looked elegant and moody. "I'm not hungry. How long has he been here?"

"A few days," Nell said. "Tyler hired him."

"And you let him stay?"

"Not voluntarily," Nell said after a minute. "I tried to bulldoze Tyler into letting him go, but he wouldn't. He wanted to know why." She lowered her eyes. "I couldn't tell him."

"Yes. I understand." She sat up suddenly, leaning her forearms on the table. "Nell, it isn't terribly bad, is it? Having him around?"

The intensity of the question was interesting. Nell smiled faintly. "No, it isn't terribly bad," she said gently. She studied the pale, beautiful features. "You still care about him, don't you?"

Margie stiffened. She actually flustered. "I...well, no, of course not. I didn't really care about him!"

"Ted has been dead for a long time," Nell said quietly. "And I'm sure he never meant for you to live without love forever. If you're asking me how I feel about Darren, he's very much like a nice stranger." She smiled gently. "I guess you and Bella were right about what happened. I blew it all out of proportion because I didn't have any experience to measure it against. I didn't exactly invite what happened, but I'd led him to believe that I wanted him without realizing it."

"It was my fault, too," Margie admitted. "But I never meant you to be hurt." She looked at the table instead of at Nell. "I cared about him. Not in the way I loved Ted, but in a different way. But I was married, and despite the way I teased him, I never would have had an affair with him."

"I know that," Nell said.

Margie smiled at her sadly. "I've spent a lot of years trying to make you over in my image, haven't I? Being bossy, taking you for granted. But I meant it in the nicest way. I wanted to help. I just didn't know how."

"I don't need help," Nell told her dryly. "And I'm not going to try to recapture the past with Darren Mc-Anders."

"And Tyler?" Margie fished. "Where does he fit in?"

That question threw her again. Was Margie infatuated with Tyler? Was her interest in Darren only pretended so that she could find out how Nell felt about Tyler? Nell started drawing into herself again, defensively. "Tyler is my foreman, nothing more. He doesn't give a hang about me in any way," Nell said tautly. She got up from the table. "I'm not hungry, Margie. I think I'll go watch TV."

"Okay. I've got to go get the boys."

"They're already on the way," Nell remarked with a bitter smile, and gestured to where Tyler was coming with both boys by the hand. They were laughing and so was he. Margie was gazing at the group with such naked hunger that Nell turned away. "See you later," she said, but Margie wasn't really listening. Her whole attention was focused on Tyler. Actually, it was focused on Darren, who was right behind Tyler, but Nell didn't see the second man. She was sure now that Margie was using Darren as an excuse to mask her feelings for Tyler.

Nell went inside and threw herself into housecleaning until she was nearly exhausted, getting rooms ready for the boys and Margie. When she came back downstairs, she was surprised to find Tyler in the living room, already watching the news.

He looked tired. Dead tired. He'd showered and changed, but he had an oblivious kind of expression on his face that brightened a little when he saw Nell come into the room.

"Can I get you a lemonade?" he asked, hoisting his.

"Not a brandy?" she mused.

"I don't drink. I never have."

She sat down in the armchair across from him, feeling her way. "Why?"

He shrugged. "I don't know. I don't like either the taste or the effect, I guess." His green eyes went over her like hands, and she flushed, because memories were glittering there. It was shocking to remember exactly how intimate he'd been with her, for all the distance that had been between them since then.

"I don't drink, either," she said absently. "I'm frightfully old-fashioned."

"Yes, I know," he said softly, and the memories were there again, warm and overwhelming. His eyes caught hers and held them relentlessly. "How do you feel about McAnders?"

She sat up straight. She had to hide her real feelings from him, so she said, "I'm not sure."

"Aren't you? You seem to spend enough time with him lately," he accused quietly.

"You spend plenty around Margie," she shot back.

He smiled mockingly. "Yes, I do, don't I? But you don't seem to spend much time considering why."

"It's obviously because she attracts you," she said haughtily. "I'm not blind."

"Oh, but you are," he said quietly. "More blind than you know."

"I can spend time with anyone I please," she continued coldly.

"Have you been intimate with McAnders?" he asked suddenly.

She gasped. Her face went bloodred as she remembered what had happened that night, what Darren had tried to do to her.

Tyler saw the expression, but he took it for guilt, and something inside him exploded. No wonder Nell had eyes for McAnders. He'd been her first love, and now he was back and he wanted her, and she'd let him touch her in all the ways Tyler had. Maybe even more. His eyes glittered at her furiously.

"How could you do that?" he asked bitterly.

She blinked. "Do what?"

He threw up his hands and paced angrily. "And all the time I thought—" He stopped short, turning. "Well, if it's McAnders you want, consider him yours. I'll run the business end of the ranch and take care of the livestock. But don't make the mistake of running after me if McAnders dumps you," he added venomously. "I don't want another man's castoff."

Nell gasped with outrage. "You lily-white purist!" she threw at him. "How many women have you cast off, if we're going to get personal?"

"That's none of your business," he said shortly.

"Well, Darren is none of yours." She clenched her hands, hating his arrogance.

He wanted to throw things. He hadn't realized until then just how deeply Nell was under his skin. He had to face the possibility that a man from her past was about to carry her off, and he didn't know what to do to stop it. She'd got the wrong end of the stick about Margie. He liked Margie, yet he saw right through her antics. But Nell was so insecure that she couldn't see the forest for the trees. Considering that insecurity it was a miracle that she could even contemplate a relationship with Darren McAnders. But she might love him....

He sighed heavily. "Fair enough," he said finally and with a long, quiet stare. "Do what you please, Nell. I won't interfere. As you say, your life is your own."

He turned to go and she felt sick all over at the way things were working out. She didn't care about Darren. She wanted to call him back and tell him the truth, but something stopped her. She couldn't tell him, she couldn't face his contempt when he knew that she'd invited Darren's advances, that she'd chased him all those years ago and brought it on herself. So she let him go, watching with sad eyes as he left the room only to run into Margie in the hall.

Nell heard him laughing and caught a glimpse of Margie's rapt expression. She couldn't bear it. She was going to lose him to Margie, and she couldn't bear it. She went back into the living room, forcing herself not to cry.

She'd let Tyler think she'd been deliberately intimate with Darren, and that was a lie. She sat down on the sofa, remembering what had happened all those years ago. She'd been mistaken about McAnders's feelings back then, and she'd become obsessed with him after he'd paid her a little attention. She recalled how she'd teased him until one night she went a little too far. Margie had given a party and that evening Nell had flirted with Mc-Anders, who'd been rejected by Margie and had had too much to drink. McAnders had come to Nell's room and found her asleep in her scanty gown, and since she hadn't locked her door, he'd thought she was waiting for him. He'd climbed into bed with her and, despite her protests, he'd been about to seduce her when Bella had come to her rescue.

But that had been years ago, long before she knew Tyler. He hadn't been talking about the past, though. He'd asked her if she'd been intimate with Darren, and he was talking about the present.

The impact of the realization hit her between the eyes like a hammer. Now she'd done it! She'd inadvertantly let him think that what she'd shared with him she'd also shared with Darren. She'd stung his pride by letting him think that she could go straight from his arms into Darren's and without a twinge of conscience.

She got up, shaking with reaction, and wondered if she could go after him, explain.

But before she got to the door, Curt and Jess came careering down the hall, and she looked past them to where Tyler was holding Margie's arm, escorting her laughingly out the front door.

It was too late now to smooth things over, she knew. She'd left it just a few seconds too long. She'd lost him.

Chapter Seven

Hi, Aunt Nell," they chorused. "Can we watch that new science fiction movie on the VCR?"

"Sure. Go ahead," she said with forced tolerance, but her heart was breaking. "Where'd your mother go?"

"Uncle Tyler's taking her into town," Curt volunteered disinterestedly as he searched for the right video-cassette. "I sure like Uncle Tyler."

"Yeah, me too," Jess agreed.

So it was "uncle" already, Nell thought, groaning inwardly. She made some brief excuse and left the room before the boys could see the tears forming in her eyes.

After that day Nell started avoiding him again. Not that it was necessary. Tyler cut her dead every time he saw her, his eyes hard and accusing, as if she'd betrayed him somehow. Nell began to wilt emotionally.

Margie and the boys left, but she and Tyler had seemed to spend a lot of time together during that visit, and Margie had been very nervous and standoffish around

Darren. So any hope Nell had that her sister-in-law might be interested in her old flame was washed away almost immediately. It was Tyler Margie wanted, and Nell didn't have a chance anymore. Not with Tyler nearly hating her for what he thought she'd done. As if she could have borne the touch of any man's hands but his; it seemed impossible that he didn't know that.

After Margie left, a morose Darren McAnders began to seek Nell out to talk about the way Margie had avoided him. He was hurt, just as she was, and their common pain brought them together as friends. She even found an odd kind of comfort in his presence.

It was an odd turn of events all around, she thought as she walked with Darren to the corral fence to see two new mares Tyler had bought. Darren was turning out to be a friend.

"You're looking moody lately," Darren remarked as they watched Chappy work one of the unbroken mares on a lunging rein. He glanced at her and smiled mischievously. "And the boss is explosive. The men are betting on how long it's going to be before he throws a punch at somebody just to let the pressure off."

She flushed. "It's complicated," she said.

He propped a boot on the lowest rail of the corral fence. "It's pretty funny for me to be offering you a shoulder to cry on, when I was your worst enemy at one time. But times have changed and so have I. And if you need somebody to listen, here I am, honey."

She looked up at him tearfully. He was different, all right. A new man altogether. She managed a smile.

He smiled back and pulled her against him to give her a friendly, totally platonic hug.

But Tyler happened to be looking out the window in the bunkhouse and he saw them. And what was a platonic hug didn't look that way to a man already trying to cope with emotions he was feeling for the first time in his life, and eaten up with unfamiliar jealousy, to boot. Tyler let out a string of range language, turned and stormed off to where he'd tied his horse. He swung up into the saddle and rode away without the slightest idea of where in hell he was going.

The square dance was the following Saturday night, and most of the present guests were leaving on Sunday to make room for a new group of people. A one-week stay was about standard for most of them. By that time they were sore enough and rested enough to go home and cope with their routines. Margie and the boys showed up Saturday afternoon, and the older woman thrust a huge box at Nell, with a mischievous smile.

"For you," she said with dancing eyes. "Open it."

Nell eyed her curiously, but she put the box on the dining room table and opened it, aware of Bella's frank interest as she did.

It was a square-dancing outfit. A red-checked full skirt with oceans of petticoats and a pretty white Mexican peasant blouse in cotton, both of which had probably cost the earth. Nell just stared at it without speaking. It was the prettiest set she'd ever seen.

"For me?" she asked Margie blankly.

"For you," came the smiling reply. "And don't put your hair up in a ponytail, will you?"

"But, Margie, I can't dance," she began.

"Wear that and someone will be sure to teach you," Margie promised.

So Nell wore the new outfit and brushed her long honey-colored hair until it shone thick and gleaming around her shoulders. Margie taught her how to put on a thin coat of makeup, and they were both surprised at the results. Nell didn't look like Nell anymore. She wasn't beautiful, but she was certainly attractive enough to make a man notice her.

Margie was wearing a similar outfit, the difference being that Margie could do anything from a square dance to a samba. Nell was too aware that she herself had at least two left feet.

Once she tried to ask Margie about Tyler, but she lost her nerve. Margie was so beautiful, and she had a way of making every man she met want her. If Tyler fell victim to her charm, who could blame him?

Nell couldn't help but wonder, though, why Margie had bought her a dress. Did she possibly sense that Nell cared about Tyler, and was trying to help her get over him by attracting Darren? But surely Margie didn't think she was interested that way in Darren, because she'd already denied it.

Downstairs, Bella made a big fuss over Nell's new image, and Nell had a feeling it was to make up for the last time she'd dressed up and Bella had been worried about Tyler getting the wrong idea. But this time praise was certainly forthcoming.

The band could be heard tuning up in the barn, which had been cleared out for the dance. Bella grinned.

"Well, at least Tyler hasn't complained about that forty dollars we have to pay the band twice a month," she said dryly.

"Give him time." Nell sighed. "Lately he complains about most everything. I hear he even made Chappy take back a rope he bought without permission."

"In case you haven't heard," Bella told Margie, "Tyler is in a snit lately. He walks around glowering at people and talking to himself."

Margie lifted an eyebrow at Nell, who flushed angrily.

"I don't have anything to do with it," Nell said shortly. "Maybe he's missing your company."

Margie exchanged glances with Bella and smiled mischievously. "Well, that's possible, of course." She eyed Nell's averted face. "Shall we go find out? Bella, you're sure you can manage the boys? They're in their pajamas, waiting for that story you promised to read them."

"Sure, me and the boys will do fine." Bella picked up a book and started toward the staircase. "Don't you worry about us."

"What are you going to read them?" Margie asked.

Bella turned and grinned wickedly. "All about the pirate raids in the Caribbean, in gory detail."

Nell gasped, but Margie laughed. "Good for you."

"Won't they have nightmares?" Nell asked.

Margie shook her head. "They love that sort of thing. I'm told that most boys do—it's normal. Their young worlds are made up of monsters and battles."

"Isn't everybody's?" Bella chuckled. "Have fun."

Nell didn't have a wrap, and it was a chilly night, but she tried not to notice the goose bumps as she and Margie walked down to the barn. Things were already in full swing, and Nell noticed that Margie's eyes were restless, as if she were looking for someone. She sighed, thinking that Margie was apparently going to single out Tyler for the evening. Nell had once been certain that Darren was the recipient of Margie's affections, but she must have been wrong.

The guests were already dancing, with Chappy calling the square dance with gleeful abandon and clapping his hands as he stood at the microphone in front of the band. Tyler was standing to one side, near the refreshment table, braiding three strands of rawhide carelessly while he glared at the dancing. He had on jeans and a blue-plaid

Western shirt, and with his black hair neatly combed and his face freshly shaven, he made Nell's heart race. He was the handsomest man she'd ever seen.

"There you are!" Margie grinned, taking possession of his arm. "How are you?"

"Fine." Tyler looked past her at Nell, glared even more at Nell, then turned his attention back to Margie. "You look like a dream, honey," he said in a tone that would have attracted bees.

"Thank you," Margie purred. She glanced at Nell. "Doesn't Nell look nice?" she added.

Nell colored and Tyler didn't say a word. He caught Margie's hand in his. "Let's get in the circle," he told her, and dragged her off without noticing the surprise in her face.

Nell moved back out of the circle of dancers and sat down in one of the chairs, feeling alone and rejected and uncomfortable. It was there that Darren found her. He was wearing a black shirt and red bandanna with his jeans, and he looked almost as handsome as Tyler but in a totally different way.

"Hi, pal," he said, smiling at Nell. "Hiding out?"

She shrugged. "I don't dance," she said with a rueful grin. "I never learned."

He cocked an eyebrow. "No time like the present," he remarked. The band had just changed to a slow, dreamy tune, and he held out his hand.

But she shook her head. "I'm not really in the mood."

He turned to look at the throng of dancers, and his face hardened when he saw Margie dancing with Tyler. He moved beside Nell to lean against one of the posts with folded arms, glaring at what he saw.

"He doesn't waste much time, does he?" he asked under his breath.

"They come from the same kind of world," Nell said quietly. "They've spent a lot of time together since he came here, and the boys love him."

"The boys don't exactly treat me like a plague victim," Darren said coldly. "Well, faint heart never won fair lady, Nell."

She smiled up at him. "In that case, good luck."

He smiled back. "Don't let him see you looking like that," he advised. "You'll blow your cover."

She sat up straighter. "God forbid."

He winked at her and moved into the dancers to tap Tyler curtly on the shoulder, nod and sweep Margie into his arms.

Tyler moved off the floor. He gave Nell a cursory glance before he picked up the rawhide strands he'd left on the corner of the refreshment table and began to braid them again.

"Lost your escort, I gather," he said coolly without looking down at her.

"What's the matter? Is the competition too much for you?" she shot back with uncharacteristic venom.

He blinked at the unfamiliar heat in her tone. His green eyes glanced over her composed features. "I thought that was your big problem, honey," he said. "Although you're dressed for it tonight."

"This old rag?" she said with a vacant smile. "Until just recently, it was the kitchen tablecloth."

He didn't smile. His eyes went to Margie and Darren, dancing like shadows, oblivious to the world.

"It's a nice crowd," Nell remarked when the silence between them lengthened.

"So it is." He finished the braid and tied it off.

"How are roundup plans coming?"

"Fine."

She took a deep breath. "My goodness, you'll talk my ear off."

"Will I?"

"You might offer to teach me to dance," she said shyly and not without reservations. Inside she was shaking as she tossed off the light remark. "You said once that you'd like it if I wore a dress, and you'd show me how."

His green eyes met hers like bullets. "Most men get poetic when they've been without a woman for a few months," he said with blunt insolence. "But you take things to heart, don't you, Nell?"

She felt the color run up her neck like fire. "I...I didn't mean..."

"Sorry, honey, but my taste doesn't run to tomboys," he said mockingly. "You might as well stick with your current favorite, if you can hold on to him. He seems to have a wandering eye."

She stood up. "That was unfair."

"Was it?" His eyes narrowed. "As for your offer, I don't want to dance with you, now or ever. And you might as well throw that—" he indicated her dress "—in the trash if you bought it to catch my eye. I'm not interested in you."

She felt the world caving in around her. She looked up at him like a small, wounded animal, tears glistening in her eyes.

She couldn't even fight back for the pain his careless words had caused. She'd had such hopes. But then, he'd made no secret of his interest in Margie. She'd been crazy to pit her charms against her sister-in-law's!

"I'm sorry!" she whispered, but her voice broke. Without another word, she turned and ran out of the barn, her skirts flying against her legs as she darted onto the porch, into the house and up the stairs. She didn't stop until she was locked in her room, and the tears came like rain.

Tyler had watched her go with anguish. He hadn't expected that reaction, especially since she'd been sitting with McAnders. Well, maybe it was the sight of Margie dancing with her lost love that had set her off that way, and not what he'd said to her at all. He had to hold on to that thought. If he started believing that what he'd said to Nell had put those tears in her eyes, he wasn't sure he could stand it.

Nell had cried herself to sleep. She woke up dry-eyed and miserable, wondering how she was going to bear it if she had to see Tyler again. Margie had come by her room last night as if she wanted to talk, but Nell had feigned sleep. She didn't know what Margie had to say, but it was probably a lot of sighing memories of Tyler and the dance, and Nell didn't want to have to listen to her.

She was only sorry that she'd shown Tyler how he'd hurt her. She never should have lost control that way. She should have thrown herself into the spirit of the dance, laughed and danced with Darren and given Tyler the cold shoulder. But she wasn't the kind of woman who could carry off that kind of charade. She wore her poor heart on her sleeve, and Tyler had crushed it.

She was surprised to find Tyler in the dining room when she went downstairs to breakfast, especially after the way they'd parted the night before.

"I want to talk to you," he began slowly.

"I can't imagine about what," she replied. She did look up then, and her dark eyes were almost black with cold rage.

"About last night," he said shortly. "I didn't mean what I said about your outfit. You looked lovely."

"Thank you," she said, but without warmth. "Last night that would have meant a lot."

"I got tired of watching you with McAnders," he admitted shortly.

She wasn't sure she'd heard him right. "Watching me with him?" she probed.

"Watching you throw yourself at him," he said with a mocking smile. "That's what it was, wasn't it? Dressing up in that fancy rig, putting on makeup. I hope he appreciated all your efforts."

She took a deep breath and felt her entire body bristling as she glared at him with her dark eyes flashing. "To be perfectly honest, I hadn't aimed my charms at Darren specifically. But thanks for the idea. Maybe I will 'throw myself' at Darren again! At least he told me I looked nice and offered to teach me to dance!"

"He felt sorry for you!" Tyler burst out without choosing his words.

"Doesn't everybody?" she shouted. "I know I'm not pretty! I'm just a stupid little tomboy who can't tell the right man from a hole in the south forty! And I'm glad he felt sorry for me—at least he didn't make fun of me!"

"Neither did I!"

"What would you call it?"

Bella came ambling into the room, her eyes like saucers, but neither of them noticed her.

"I got the wrong end of the stick!" he tried to explain.

"Well, why don't you get hold of the right end?" she invited. "And I'll tell you exactly where you can put it and how far!"

"Nell!" Bella burst out, shocked.

"If that's how you feel, we'll drop the whole subject," Tyler said through his teeth. One lean hand was almost crushing the brim of his hat, but he seemed to be beyond noticing it.

"Good! Why don't you go out and ride a horse or something?"

"You won't even listen . . . !"

"I did listen!" Nell raged, red faced. "You said I might as well throw my clothes in the trash as wear them to impress you, that you weren't interested and that I took things to heart . . . !"

"Oh, God!" he groaned.

"And that it was just abstinence that was responsible for everything!" she concluded fiercely. "Well, that works both ways, cowboy! And you can get out of my dining room. You're curdling my eggs!"

His face was like rock, and his eyes blazed up like green fires. "Damn your eggs! Will you listen?"

"I will not, and I'm not eating the damned eggs. Here, you can have them, and welcome!" And she flung the plate at him, eggs and all, and stalked out of the room.

Tyler stood there, quite still, with egg literally on his face, his shirt, his jeans. A piece of egg had even landed in his hat.

Bella cocked her head warily as she waited for the explosion. He glared at her for a minute and deliberately stuck the hat on his head.

"Would you, uh, like some bacon to go with your eggs?" she asked.

"No, thanks," he said calmly. "I don't really have anyplace left to put it."

He turned and walked out, and Bella was hard put not to collapse with hysteria. Imagine, Nell actually shouting at anybody! That young lady was definitely getting herself together, and Tyler was going to be in for some hard times if Bella didn't miss her guess.

The cold war had truly begun. Nell sent messages to Tyler by Chappy during roundup and she never went near the holding pens. The most she did was to call Bob Wyler about the helicopter and make arrangements with the transport people to get the calves to the auction barn. Otherwise, she busied herself with the guests, who were enjoying the warm autumn climate and especially the cookouts and trail drives that Nell led herself.

Her confidence was beginning to grow, except where Tyler Jacobs was concerned. She felt like a new woman. She discarded her old wardrobe and bought a new one. This time, she bought jeans that fit and tops that clung. She had her hair trimmed and shaped. She began to wear makeup. And she learned from Margie how to gracefully get out of potentially disturbing situations with male guests without hard feelings. She was beginning to bloom, like a delayed spring flower blossoming before winter.

Margie began spending more and more time at the ranch, and every time Nell looked out, she saw her sister-in-law with Tyler. Darren grew moody and frankly angry, and began cutting at Margie every time he saw her. She cut back. It got to the point that they were avoiding each other like the plague, but Tyler seemed to benefit from that, because Margie spent most all her time with him. He enjoyed it, too, if the expression on his face and in his eyes was anything to go by. The boys had even started teasing them about their preoccupation with each other. But it was a loving kind of teasing, because the boys were crazy about Tyler. Darren had captured at least some of their attention during the frequent visits, though, because they began to seek him out to show them about horses and cattle and tell them stories he'd heard from his grandfather about the old days in the West. That irri-

tated Margie, but she couldn't make them stop following Darren around. And Tyler wouldn't. That, too, was
puzzling to Nell.

Meanwhile, Tyler was becoming more and more unapproachable. He glared daggers through Nell when she
was looking, and watched her hungrily when she wasn't.
Bella knew, but she kept her mouth shut. It wouldn't do
to interfere, she reckoned. Things had a way of working
out better without meddling from interested bystanders.
She'd learned her lesson.

Roundup ended and the calves brought a better than
expected price at auction, which pleased Uncle Ted no
end. He praised Nell for the way things were going at the
ranch and then asked with elaborate carelessness what she
thought of his foreman.

Nell made an excuse to get off the phone without an-
swering the question. It was too hard thinking up nice
ways to tell her uncle that she thought his foreman would
be best barbecued.

She'd no sooner hung up than the phone rang again.
She picked it up. The voice on the line was a woman's and
unfamiliar.

"Is this Nell Regan?" she was asked hesitantly.

"Yes."

"I'm Shelby Jacobs Ballenger," came the quiet reply.
"I was hoping that I might be able to speak to my
brother."

Nell sat down. "He's gone into town to pick up some
supplies," she said, remembering the fondness Tyler's
voice had betrayed when he mentioned his only relative,
his sister, Shelby. "But he'll be back within the hour. Can
I have him call you?"

"Oh, dear." Shelby sighed. "Justin and I are leaving
for Jacobsville in just a few hours. We're just in Tucson

on a quick business trip, and I was hoping that we could see him." She laughed self-consciously. "You see, he's been worried about me. Justin and I got off to a rocky start, but things are wonderful now and I wanted him to see us together, so that he'd be sure I was telling him the truth."

"Why don't you come down here," Nell offered impulsively. "We're only about thirty minutes out of Tucson. Have you a car?"

"Yes, Justin rented one for his meeting. It would be all right? You wouldn't mind having two strangers barge in on you?"

"You're not a stranger," Nell said with a smile. "Tyler's talked about you so much that we all feel as if we know you. We'd love for you to come. Bella can make a cake—"

"Oh, please, don't go to any trouble."

"It's no trouble, really. You just come on down." And she proceeded to give Shelby directions. Although God only knew why she should go to so much effort to give Tyler a nice surprise when he'd been simply horrible to her. It must have been a touch too much sun, she decided after she'd hung up.

"Tyler's sister, coming here?" Bella grinned from ear to ear. "I'll go bake a nice chocolate cake. You tidy up the living room."

Nell glowered. "It's already tidy."

"Good. Then lay a tray and make sure the silver's nice and polished."

Nell threw up her hands. "Botheration!"

"It was your idea to have them come down," she was reminded. Bella smiled with sickening superiority. "What a sweet surprise for Tyler. And here I thought you hated him. Slinging scrambled eggs all over him, yelling at him..."

"I'll just see about that silver," Nell murmured, and got out of Bella's sight.

A little more than half an hour later, a rented limousine pulled up at the sidewalk and two people got out. Nell recognized Shelby Jacobs Ballenger almost at once, because she looked so much like her brother. She was lovely, very slender and tall and elegant with her dark hair in a French twist and wearing a green silk dress. She was no surprise, but the tall man with her was. He was very masculine, that was apparent, but he wasn't handsome at all, and he looked as if he didn't smile much. Nell felt immediately intimidated and tried not to show it when she went to the door to greet them.

"You have to be Nell." Shelby smiled. She reached forward and hugged the younger woman warmly. "It's so nice to meet you. I'm Shelby, and this is Justin." She looked up at the tall man, her expression full of love.

He smiled back at her for an instant and then diverted his lancing dark gaze to Nell. "Nice to meet you."

Nell nodded, tongue-tied, she was glad that she'd put on clean jeans and a nice blue-checked blouse and brushed her hair. At least she didn't look scruffy.

She led them into the living room and Bella came in to be introduced, carrying a coffee tray laden with the necessities and a platter of fresh chocolate cake.

"My favorite," Justin murmured, grinning at Bella. "Thank you, but what are they going to eat?" he asked with an innocent glance at the women.

The ice was immediately broken. Nell relaxed visibly and sat down to pour coffee.

"When Tyler comes, waylay him and send him in, but don't tell him why," Nell called to Bella.

"I'll tell him you want to give him some more eggs," Bella said smugly and left the room.

Nell's color intrigued Shelby, who stirred cream into her coffee absently and began to smile. "Eggs?" she probed.

Nell cleared her throat. "We had an, er, slight misunderstanding."

"Eggs?" Justin asked, looking dryly interested.

It was getting more uncomfortable by the second. "I sort of lost my temper and threw my breakfast at him," Nell confessed. She looked at Shelby pleadingly. "Well, he insulted me first."

"Oh, I can believe that." Shelby nodded, smiling. "I'm not going to put all the blame on you."

"How's he fitting in here?" Justin asked as he leaned back against the sofa with his coffee cup in one hand.

"He fits in fine with the men," Nell said restlessly. Justin's dark eyes were piercing, and they didn't seem to miss much.

Shelby was watching her just as closely, and with a faintly amused smile. "You know," she said, "you don't seem anything like Tyler's description of you at my wedding."

Nell cleared her throat. "Am I better or worse?" she asked.

"If you answer that, I'll disown you," came Tyler's deep voice from the doorway.

"Ty!" Shelby got up and ran into his arms, to be swung high and kissed while he smiled in a way Nell had never seen him smile. It made her see what she'd missed, and it made her sad.

"Good to see you again," Justin said, rising to shake hands with Tyler before he drew Shelby close to his side.

That simple gesture told Tyler how things were between the recently married couple. Justin looked at her with open possessiveness, and Shelby stayed as close to him as she could get. Apparently they'd solved their difficulties, because no couple could pretend the kind of explosive emotion that crackled between them like electricity. Tyler relaxed, sure of Shelby's future. That was one load off his mind. He'd been worried about the marriage's rocky start.

"We thought we'd call you before we left Tucson," Shelby explained while they drank coffee and ate chocolate cake. "But Nell invited us down to see you before we fly home to Texas."

"Nice of her, wasn't it?" Justin asked with that smug, lazy smile that made Tyler's neck hair bristle.

"Nice," Tyler said shortly. He didn't look at Nell, who was sitting in an armchair while he shared the sofa with Shelby and Justin.

"Don't strain yourself thanking me," Nell said with venomous politeness. "I'd have done the same thing for anyone."

Tyler's green eyes glittered at her across the coffee table. "I'm sure you would, you tender-hearted little thing."

He said it with deep sarcasm and Nell stiffened. "I used to have a tender heart all right," she told him flatly, "but I wore it out on men."

"That's right," he invited, "put all the blame on us. Men can't put a foot right where you're concerned, can they?"

"They can if they have a woman to lead them," Nell said, and smiled icily.

"Let me tell you, I won't live long enough to let a woman lead me anywhere! Furthermore…" He stopped, clearing his throat gruffly when he noticed the attention he was getting from the visitors. He smiled. "How are things back in Jacobsville?" he asked with pleasant interest.

It was to Justin's credit that he didn't fall on the floor laughing when he tried to answer that. Meanwhile, Shelby smiled into her coffee and exchanged a highly amused glance with her husband. They didn't need a program to see what was going on. It looked very much to Shelby as if Tyler had met his match, and not a minute too soon.

Chapter Eight

Shelby and Justin stayed for another half hour, giving Tyler some interesting news from back home. Justin's brother, Calhoun, and sister-in-law, Abby, had flown to Europe for a belated honeymoon, and a neighbor had bought Geronimo, Tyler's prize stud stallion.

"I'm glad Harrison got him," Tyler murmured, his face faintly bitter because the remark reminded him of all he and Shelby had lost. "He was a good horse."

"He'll be well taken care of," Shelby added. "I'll make sure of it." She smiled at her brother. "Don't brood over it, will you? We can't do anything about the past."

Justin saw storm clouds coming and quickly headed them off. "I hate to cut this short," he said with a glance at his thin gold watch, "but we've got to go, honey."

Shelby clung to Justin's hand as they stood up, releasing it for just a minute while she hugged Tyler and then Nell. "Thanks for letting us come, Nell. Ty, try to write

once in a while, or at least call and let us know you're
alive."

He smiled at his sister. "I'll do my best. Take good care
of her, Justin."

"Oh, that's the easy part," Justin said, and his
expression as he smiled at his wife was loving and possessive and very sexy. Justin might look formidable, but
Nell had a feeling he shared with Shelby a side of himself that no one else would ever see. That was what marriage should be, Nell thought. Not that she was ever
going to have a chance at it.

She walked to the door with Tyler to see Justin and
Shelby off. It was already dusk and getting darker by the
minute. In the distance, the guest houses were all alight
and there was the sound of a guitar and a harmonica
playing down at the bunkhouse. Nell wrapped her arms
around herself, reluctant to leave Tyler, but too nervous
of him to stay.

She turned, only to find his hand sliding down to grasp
hers.

"Not yet," he said, and there was a familiar deep note
in his voice.

She should have had more willpower, but things had
been strained between them for too long already, and the
touch of his hand on hers made her weak.

"Come for a walk with me, Nell," he said quietly, and
drew her along with him down the path that led to his
cabin.

Even as she went along, she knew that she shouldn't
go. He was leading up to a confrontation. But the night
was perfumed with flowers, and the stars were above
them, and silence drew around them like a dark blanket.
His hand in hers was warm against the chill of the desert
night, and she moved closer, feeling the strength of his

body like a shield at her side. She sensed his sadness and bitterness, and all the hostility fell away from her. He needed someone to talk to; that was probably all he wanted. She understood that. She'd never had anyone who she could really talk to, until Darren McAnders had come back and become her friend. But she'd much rather have talked to Tyler. She couldn't do anything to change his past, but she could certainly listen.

He stopped at the corral fence and let go of her hand to light a cigarette while they listened to the night sounds and the silences.

"I like your sister," she said softly.

"So do I. She and I have been close all our lives. All we ever really had was each other when we were growing up. After our mother died, our father became greedy and grasping. He was hell to live with most of the time, and he wasn't above blackmail."

"Have she and Justin known each other a long time?" she asked curiously.

"Years." He took a draw of the cigarette, and his smile was reflected by the orange glow from its tip. "Six years ago they got engaged, but Shelby ended it. I never knew why, although I'm sure my father had a hand in it. Justin wasn't wealthy and Dad had just the right rich man picked out for Shelby. She didn't marry anyone as it turned out. Then when we lost everything, Justin went to see her because she had no one—I'd just come out here to work. And the next thing we knew, they were married. I thought he'd done that for revenge, that he was going to make her life miserable. She didn't seem very happy on their wedding day." He glanced down at her. "But I think they've worked things out. Did you notice the way they look at each other?"

Nell leaned against the fence and kept her face down. "Yes. They seem to be very happy."

"And very lucky. Most people don't get a second chance."

She lifted her eyes. "If that's a dig at me because I've avoided you since the square dance..."

"I was jealous, Nell," he said unexpectedly. He smiled faintly at the stunned expression on her face that was barely visible in the dim light from the house. "Jealous as hell. I'd seen you and McAnders in a clinch, and then you dressed up for him, I thought, when you'd never dressed up for me. I just blew up. I didn't really mean the things I said to you, but you wouldn't listen when I tried to explain."

"Jealous of me?" She laughed bitterly. "That'll be the day. I'm a tomboy, I'm plain, I'm shy—"

"And sadly lacking in self-confidence," he finished for her. "Don't you think that a man could want you for yourself? For the things you are instead of how you look?"

"Nobody ever has," she said shortly. "I'm twenty-four and I'll die an old maid."

"Not you, honey," he said softly. "You're too passionate to live and die alone."

Her face went hot. "Don't throw that up to me," she snapped, her eyes flashing. "I was...I was off balance and you're too experienced for me, that's all."

"Experienced, hell," he said shortly. "There haven't even been that many women, and you weren't off balance—you were starved for a little love."

"Thanks a lot!"

"Will you just shut up and listen?" he demanded. "You never would give me a chance to say anything about what happened, you just slung scrambled eggs at me and stomped off in a fury."

"I was entitled to be angry after what you said to me," she reminded him curtly.

"Oh, hell, maybe you were," he conceded tautly. "But you could have let me explain."

"The explanation was obvious," she replied. "Darren was poaching on what you considered your territory."

He smiled in spite of himself. "You might say that."

"Well, you don't have to worry about Margie," she said after a minute. "I mean, it's obvious that she's crazy about you. And the boys like you...."

"What are you talking about?" he asked pleasantly.

"Nobody could blame you for being attracted to her," she went on. "And I'm sorry if I've made things difficult for you—I didn't mean to. You've lost so much. You should have somebody to care about. Somebody who'll care about you."

"Coals of fire," he murmured, watching her as he smoked his cigarette. "Do you want me to be happy, Nell?"

"I want that very much," she said, her voice soft in the darkness. "I haven't meant to be difficult. It's just..."

"You don't have a scrap of self-confidence, that's just what it is," he said for her. "That's a shame, Nell, because you've got a lot going for you. I wish I knew why you had this hang-up about men."

"I got hurt once," she muttered.

"Most people get hurt once."

"Not like I did." She folded her arms across her breasts. "When I was in my middle teens, I had a terrible crush on one of the cowboys. I plagued him and followed him around and chased him mercilessly. To make a long story short, he was in love with a woman he couldn't have, and in a drunken stupor he decided to take me up on my offer.'' She laughed bitterly. ''Until then, I had no idea that romance was anything except smiling at each other and maybe holding hands. It never actually occurred to me that people in love went to bed together. And what made it so bad was that physically I didn't feel anything for him. I guess that's why I panicked and screamed. Bella came and rescued me and the cowboy left in disgrace.''

Tyler had listened intently. The cigarette burned away between his fingers without his noticing. ''It was Mc-Anders,'' he guessed with cold certainty.

''Yes. He was in love with Marguerite, but I didn't know it until he tried to make love to me. I realized that night what a terrible mistake I'd made.'' She smiled halfheartedly. ''So then I knew that I couldn't trust my instincts or my judgment anymore. I stopped wearing sexy clothes and I stopped running after anybody.''

''One bad egg doesn't make the whole carton spoil,'' he said.

''That's true, but how do you find the bad egg in time?'' She shook her head. ''I've never had the inclination to try again.''

''Until I came along?''

She flushed. ''I told you, I was only trying to make you feel welcome. You paid me a little attention and it flattered me.''

''Where does McAnders fit into this now?'' he asked. ''I gather that you were fairly intimate with him before Bella came to the rescue, but how about today? Did you go from me to him?''

She shifted restlessly. ''No,'' she said under her breath.

He brightened a little. ''Why not?''

She had to remember that he was interested in Margie, not her. He might feel a little sorry for her, but he didn't want her for keeps. She straightened. "He still doesn't appeal to me physically."

He wondered if she realized what she was giving away with that remark. If she didn't want McAnders she probably didn't really love him. But he was going to have to make her see that, and it wouldn't be easy.

"I appealed to you physically, once," he said gently, his voice deep and drugging in the still night. He moved closer, his fingers lightly touching her face, her loosened hair. His warmth enveloped her, his breath was like a faint breeze, moving the hair at her temples, making her heart race. "If McAnders hadn't shown up, I might have appealed to you in other ways. We didn't have enough time to get to know each other."

She put her hands slowly, flatly against his shirtfront, hesitating as if she thought he might throw them away. But he caught them gently and pressed them to the soft cotton of his shirt.

"You wouldn't want to, now," she said, and her voice shook. "Margie's here half the time."

"And, of course, you think I'm madly in love with her."

"Aren't you?" she asked stubbornly.

"I'm not going to tell you that," he said. He lifted her chin. "You're going to have to come out of your shell, little one, and start looking around you. You can't learn to swim if you keep balking at the water."

"I don't understand."

"Very simply, Nell, if you want me, you're going to have to believe that I can want you back. You're going to have to believe in yourself a little and start trusting me not to hurt you."

"Trust comes hard," she said, although what he was saying was more tempting than he realized. She did want him, terribly, but she was playing for keeps. Was he?

"It comes hard to most people." He smoothed the hair away from her face. "It depends on whether or not you think it's worth the chance. Love doesn't come with a money-back guarantee. There comes a time when you have to trust your instincts and take a chance."

She shifted restlessly, but he wouldn't let go of her hands. "Why?" she asked abruptly. "You said you wanted me, but at the same time you said you weren't interested in any relationships with women."

"I said a lot, didn't I, honey?" he murmured dryly.

She searched what she could see of his dark face. "I'm not the kind of woman you could care about," she said miserably.

"My whole life has turned upside down, Nell," he told her. "I'm not the same man I used to be. I don't have wealth or position, and about all that's left is my good name and a lot of credit. That makes me pretty vulnerable, in case you've missed it."

"Vulnerable, how?" she asked.

"You might think I was interested in you because you're a woman of property."

"That'll be the day," she murmured dryly. "There's no way I can see you chasing a woman for her money."

His quiet eyes pierced the darkness, looking for her face. "At least you know me that well," he said. "But part of you is afraid of me."

"You want Marguerite," she moaned. "Why bother with me?"

"Margie sends out signals. You could learn to do that, too," he said conversationally. "You could waylay me in the office and kiss me stupid, or buy a new wardrobe to dazzle me with.''

She blushed and her heart jumped into her throat. ''Fat chance when you made Chappy take back a rope he bought,'' she reminded him to lighten the tension that was growing between them.

He grinned. ''Buy a new dress. I promise not to fuss.''

''Margie bought me a new dress and you made me feel dowdy when I wore it,'' she said.

''Yes, I know.'' He sighed. ''I keep trying to apologize, but you don't hear me.''

Her heart was running wild; while he spoke his hands had gone to her hips and pulled them slowly to his. She tried to step back, but he held her there very gently.

''No,'' he said softly. ''You can't run away this time. I won't let you.''

''I have to go inside,'' she said. Panic was rising in her at the intimacy of his hold. It was bringing back dangerously sweet memories.

''Frightened, Nell?'' he asked quietly.

''I won't be just another conquest!'' she groaned, struggling.

''Stand still, for God's sake.'' He gasped suddenly, and his powerful body stiffened. ''God, Nell, that hurts!''

She stopped instantly. Her color was rising when she felt what he was talking about and realized that she was only complicating things.

''Then you shouldn't hold me like this,'' she whispered shakily.

He took a steadying breath and his hands contracted on her waist. ''We've been a lot closer, though, haven't we?'' he asked at her forehead, brushing his lips against her skin. ''We've been together without a scrap of fabric between your breasts and my chest, and you pulled my head down and arched up to meet my mouth.''

She buried her embarrassed face in his shirt, shaking with remembered pleasure. ''I shouldn't have let you,'' she whispered.

''Then Chappy came to the door and broke the spell,'' he murmured at her cheek. ''I didn't want to answer it. I wanted to go on loving you. But I guess it was a good thing he came along, because things were getting out of hand, weren't they? We wanted each other so much, Nell. I don't really know that we could have stopped in time.''

He was right. That didn't make her guilt any easier to bear. ''And that would have been a disaster, wouldn't it?'' she asked, waiting stiffly for his answer.

''I'm an old-fashioned man, honey,'' he said finally. His hands smoothed down her back, holding her against him. ''I wouldn't ask you to sleep with me, knowing that you're a virgin. You aren't that kind of woman.''

She bit her lower lip hard. ''I've got all these hang-ups...''

''Most of which we removed that day in my bed,'' he reminded her. ''But your biggest hang-up, little Nell, is your mental block about your attractions. You're the only person around here who doesn't see what a dish you are.''

''Me?'' she asked breathlessly.

''You.'' He bent to her mouth and brushed it with his. ''You've got a warm heart,'' he whispered, bending again. The kiss lingered this time, just a second longer. ''You're caring.'' He kissed her again, and this time he parted her lips briefly before he raised his head. ''You're intelligent.'' His mouth teased, brushing hers open breath by breath. ''And you're the sexiest woman I've ever made love to...''

He whispered the words into her trembling lips before he took them, and this time he didn't draw back. His tongue began to penetrate her mouth in slow, exquisite thrusts. This was a kind of kiss Nell hadn't experienced before, not even that day in Tyler's cabin, and she was afraid of it.

She tried to draw back, but his lean hand at her nape held her mouth under his.

"Don't fight it," he whispered coaxingly. "I won't hurt you. Relax, Nell. Let me have your mouth. I'll treat it just as tenderly as I'd treat your body if you gave yourself to me, little one," he breathed, and his mouth whispered down onto hers.

The words in addition to the expert teasing of his tongue shook away every last bit of her reserve. She melted into the length of him, trembling with the fierce hunger he was arousing in her body. She moaned helplessly and felt his mouth smile against hers. Then he deepened the pressure and the slow thrust of his tongue into the sweet, soft darkness of her mouth.

But what about Margie? she wanted to ask. How can you hold me like this when you want her? She couldn't have asked him that to save her life, because he was working magic on her body. She wanted him. Tomorrow she could hate herself and him for leading her on, for toying with her. But tonight she wanted nothing except the sweet pleasure of his mouth and his hands and a few memories to carry through the long years ahead.

She felt his hands at the back of her thighs, pulling her shaking legs closer so that her hips were grinding into his, so that she knew how aroused he was. She didn't protest. Her hands found their way around him, to his back and down, returning the pressure shyly even as the first shudder of desire ripped through her and dragged a cry from her lips.

He lifted his head abruptly. His eyes glittered and he was trembling a little; his heartbeat was rough against her breasts. "Come home with me. I'll sit with you in that big leather armchair by the fireplace, and we'll love each other for a few minutes."

She was crying with reaction. "It's so dangerous," she pleaded, but it was no protest at all, and he had to know it.

"I've got to, Nell," he whispered, bending to lift her so gently into his arms. He turned, carrying her the rest of the way to his porch in the darkness. "I've got to, sweetheart."

Her arms went around his neck, and she buried her face in his warm, pulsating throat. "I can't...I can't sleep with you," she whispered.

"I'd never ask that of you," he breathed ardently. He caught her mouth hungrily with his while he fumbled the door open with one hand and carried her into the dark stillness of his cabin.

He kicked the door shut and moved to the big armchair, dropping into it with his mouth still hard and sure on her lips.

There was no more pretense left. He was hungry and he wasn't trying to hide it. He fought the buttons of her blouse out of his way and deftly removed it and the lacy covering beneath. His mouth found her warm breasts, and he nuzzled them hungrily, nibbling, kissing, tasting while she shuddered and arched her back to help him.

"So sweet, Nell," he groaned as his lips moved on her. "Oh, God, you taste like honey in my mouth."

Her hands touched his cool dark hair, savoring its clean thickness while she fed on the aching sweetness of his mouth. "Oh, please!" she moaned brokenly when he lifted his head to breathe. "Tyler, please . . . !"

He held her quietly while he tore open the snaps of his own shirt and dragged her inside it, pressing her breasts against the hair-covered warmth of his chest, moving her sensually from side to side so that her breathing became as rough and torturous as his own.

His mouth ground into hers then, rough with need, his restraint gone, his control broken by the sounds she was making against his lips, by the helpless movement of her body against him, silky and bare and terribly arousing.

His lean hands caressed her soft, bare back, holding her to him so that he could feel the hard tips of her breasts like tiny brands on his skin.

"Nell," he groaned. His mouth slid away from hers and into her throat, pressing hard against the wildly throbbing artery as he drew her up close and held her, rocked her, until the trembling need began to drain out of her.

"I ache all over," she whispered with tears in her voice. She clung closer. "Tyler, this is scary!"

"This is desire," he breathed at her ear, and his arms contracted. "This is the raw need to mate. Don't be afraid of it. I'm not going to take advantage of something you can't help. I want you just as much as you want me."

She shuddered helplessly. "It must be . . . so much worse for you," she whispered.

"A sweet ache," he confessed huskily, and his mouth brushed her cheek, her throat. "I don't have a single regret. Do you?"

"I shouldn't admit it."

He chuckled, delighted with her headlong response to him, with her helpless hunger. "Neither should I. But wasn't it good, Nell? Wasn't it delicious?"

"Oh, yes." She sighed, nestling closer with a tiny sound deep in her throat. "I want to stay with you all night."

"I want that, too, but we can't."

"I could just sleep with you," she murmured drowsily.

"Sure you could. Platonically. And nothing would happen." He turned up her face and kissed her mouth hard. "You know as well as I do that we'd devour each other if we got into a bed together. We're half-crazy to be together already, and I've barely touched you."

She pulled back a little. "You call that barely touching?" she asked, awed.

"Compared to what I'd do to you in bed, yes."

She hesitated, but he read the thought in her mind and chuckled helplessly.

"Shall I tell you?" he whispered softly.

"You wouldn't dare."

But he would. And he did, sensuously, whispering it into her ear while he touched her, lightly caressed her, brought every nerve in her body to singing, agonizing pleasure.

"I never dreamed . . . !" she gasped, hiding her face in his chest when he finished.

"You needed to know," he said gently. "You're still very innocent, despite what happened in your teens. I want you to understand that what you and I would share wouldn't be painful or frightening. Physical love is an expression of what two people feel for each other so strongly that words aren't enough to contain it. It isn't anything to dread."

"Certainly not with you it wouldn't be," she said tenderly. She touched his hard face, loving its strength, its masculine beauty. "Tyler...I could love you," she whispered hesitantly.

"Could you, honey?" He bent, brushing his mouth with exquisite softness against her lips. "If you want me, Nell, come after me."

"That isn't fair," she began.

"It's fair," he said. "For your own peace of mind, you need to regain the confidence you lost because of what happened with McAnders. Oh, I could back you into a corner and force you into a decision, but that would rob you of your right to choose. I won't do it for you. You have to do it, alone."

Her worried eyes studied his profile. "You said you didn't want a lasting relationship...." she said again.

He turned his head and looked down at her in the dimness of the unlit room. "Make me want one," he challenged. "Vamp me. Buy some sexy dresses and drive me crazy. Be the woman you can be. The woman you should have been."

"I'm not attractive," she argued faintly.

His hand swept slowly, lovingly, over her breasts. "You're beautiful, Nell," he said huskily. "Firm and soft and silky to touch."

"Tyler..."

"Come here," he groaned. He stood up with her in his arms and let her slide down his body, bent to kiss her hungrily before his hand shot out and fumbled with a light switch.

"No!" she protested, but it was too late. The soft light flooded the living room, and Tyler caught her hands before she could cover herself. He gazed down at her with an intent masculine appreciation of her attributes, which brought a wave of color up her neck and into her face. His chest rose and fell heavily, and his expression showed that he was having a monumental battle with his conscience to do nothing more than look.

"I'll live on this for a while," he breathed, lifting his eyes to hers.

Her lips parted as she stared back at him, all too aware of the tense swelling of her breasts, of their hard arousal, which he could see as well as feel.

"It embarrasses you, doesn't it?" he asked softly, searching her eyes. "I can see how lovely you are, how aroused I've made you. It's like letting me see you totally nude, isn't it? But you've seen me that way already, Nell. Remember?"

She lowered her eyes to his bare chest. "I couldn't forget if I tried. I thought you were perfect," she whispered shyly.

"I feel just that way about you. I love the way you look without your blouse. I'd give everything I have to carry you into my bedroom and love you in my bed. But as things stand, that's a decision I can't make." He let go of her hands and gazed at her one last time before he forced himself to turn his back and light a cigarette. "You'd better dress, sweetheart. I want you desperately right now, and I'm not quite as controlled as I thought I was."

She stared at his back for an instant, thinking of pressing herself against him. But she knew what would happen, and it would be her fault. She sighed softly and went to find her blouse and bra.

He got into his shirt and buttoned it and smoked half his cigarette before he turned around again. His eyes were dark with frustrated hunger as he looked at her. "We can't do much of that," he said with a tender smile. "It gets worse every time."

"Yes." She smiled back. "Oh, I want you so," she whispered helplessly.

"I want you, too." He held out his hand, and she put hers into it without hesitation. "I'd better walk you home."

"All right."

He went with her up the path in the darkness. He didn't speak and neither did she, but she clung to his hand and felt as if they'd become lovers in every sense of the word. There would never be, could never be, anyone after him. She felt that with a sense of faint despair, because she still didn't know where she stood with him.

He stopped at the front steps and turned her. His face was clearly visible in the light pouring out the window from the front room.

"No more pretense, Nell," he said softly. "If you want me, show me."

"But men don't like being chased," she whispered.

"Try it and see," he challenged with narrowed eyes. "You've got to believe in yourself before other people will."

"You won't mind?" she asked. "You're sure?"

He bent and put his mouth warmly against hers in a brief kiss. "I won't mind."

"But what about Margie?" she groaned.

"You'll find out about that all by yourself when you start putting your life back in order," he said simply. "It's right under your nose, but you just can't see it."

"Tell me," she whispered.

"No. You work it out. Good night, Nell."

Impulsively she moved closer and lifted her mouth. "Would you . . . kiss me again?" she whispered.

He did, half lifting her against him, and so thoroughly and hungrily that when he let her down again, she gasped.

"I like that," he said roughly. "You might try it again from time to time. Sleep well."

"You, too." She watched him turn and walk back the way they'd come, lighting a cigarette on the way. His stride was moody and thoughtful, but as she turned to go in, she heard him whistling a light, cheerful tune in the darkness. She smiled, because it was a popular love song. She knew that she might be reading too much into what they'd done, but her heart was on fire for him. Maybe he didn't really care that much about Margie. Maybe she could worm her way into his affection if she tried. But it was going to take some hard thinking before she risked her heart again. She needed time.

Chapter Nine

Nell worried all night about Margie and Tyler and what she was going to do. Her own insecurities haunted her.

She went downstairs, her thoughts murky and still without concrete answers. She half expected Tyler to be there again, waiting for her, but he wasn't.

Bella bustled in with breakfast and sat down beside Nell. "Too early for the new arrivals to be up and hungry, so you and I can have ours in peace," she said, pouring two cups of coffee. "Tyler's having his in the bunkhouse."

"That's nothing unusual, is it?" Nell sighed. "He always seems to be eating down there lately."

"I don't think he's felt very welcome here in recent days," Bella told her bluntly. "Pity, because he sure is a nice fella and you could do worse."

"It isn't me he wants," Nell said curtly, glaring at the older woman as she helped herself to a fresh biscuit and buttered it. "It's Margie."

Bella sipped her coffee. "Did he tell you that?"

"No. But he didn't deny it, either."

The older woman spooned scrambled eggs onto her plate and reached for bacon. "Nell, I steered you wrong when Tyler came here. I should have encouraged you to dress up and act like a young lady. I should have realized what kind of man he was. But I didn't, and I've helped complicate things. I'm sorry."

"You didn't do anything," Nell said. She glowered at her eggs. "I'm not the kind of woman a man like Tyler needs. I'm just a country tomboy. I don't even know how to dance."

"Stop running yourself down," Bella said gruffly. "Listen, child, just because Darren McAnders couldn't see past Margie to you is no reason for you to bury yourself in baggy britches forever. You're young and pretty, and if you tried, you could be everything Tyler needs. Don't forget, he isn't a rich man anymore. He doesn't need a social butterfly, he needs a woman who can help him build a new legacy for his children."

"Margie can work," Nell said halfheartedly.

"Oh, sure, like she does when she's here?" Bella scoffed. "Fat chance. Tyler would be out of his mind after the first week and you know it. She'd never cook supper—she'd be too busy trying on dresses in town or gossiping on the telephone."

"She's pretty and flamboyant."

"A sensible man doesn't want a wall decoration, he wants a flesh-and-blood woman."

"I guess I'm flesh and blood," Nell agreed.

"And a hard worker, a good little cook, and a companion who listens more than she talks. You're a jewel," Bella concluded. "You should think positively. At least you've made a start. You're wearing clothes that really fit, and you've put away that horrible slouchy hat and let your hair down. You look like a different Nell."

"I decided that you and Margie were right about what happened with Darren," she conceded. "I overreacted because I didn't know what a man was like when he was hungry for a woman. Well, not then, at least."

Bella's eyes widened. "And now you do?" she asked with a slow, wicked smile.

Nell felt the flush working its way up her neck. She reached blindly for her coffee and turned it over onto the tablecloth and herself.

"Oh, my, what little fumble fingers." Bella chuckled.

"I meant to do that," Nell protested as she got to her feet, brushing at a tiny spot on her blue-checked Western shirt and her new jeans. She glared at Bella. "I just hate coffee. And I don't fumble!" she added.

Then she turned around and tripped over the chair and fell flat on her face.

Bella doubled over laughing while Nell, bruised and furious, disentangled herself from the chair. She was turning the air blue when she saw a pair of boots come into view past her nose.

"She don't fumble," Bella explained to the boots, and walked off into the kitchen.

Nell scrambled to her feet, assisted by a familiar lean strong hand.

"Having trouble?" Tyler asked pleasantly.

She did fumble then, nervous with him and still uncertain of her ground. She looked up into his dark face, wondering at the secret pleasure it gave her just to stare at him.

"I was looking for a contact lens," Nell said, flustered.

"You don't wear contact lenses," he pointed out.

She cleared her throat. "That doesn't mean that I can't look for one if I want to."

He smiled slowly. "Whatever turns you on," he said dryly.

She brushed back her unruly hair. "What can I do for you?" she asked abruptly.

"You can come on the camp out trail ride with me this afternoon," he said. "Chappy's tied up with those new mares, so I told him we'd take the greenhorns out today."

She colored. "You and not Darren?"

He pursed his lips. "That's right. Is that a problem?" he added quietly.

She was still feeling her way, but telling the truth might be a good start, she decided. "No, it's not a problem," she said. "Darren has been a good friend. But I'd rather be with you."

He smiled slowly because her face flamed when she said it, and her shyness made her even more delectable to him. She was a pretty woman when she didn't dress like a baggy orphan.

"I'd rather be with you, too, sunshine," he said softly.

Her heart soared. Heaven must be this sweet, she thought dazedly. She smiled at him, her dark eyes like brown velvet.

Bella came through the door and broke the spell. Nell excused herself as the housekeeper giggled wickedly, and went out into the hall to get her hat. She did her usual chores, feeling as if she were walking on air, and the day was all too long until it was time to pack the bedrolls and the cooking utensils and the food that Bella had provided and head out for an overnight camp out. The Double R Ranch was one of the few left that did it for real, complete with bedrolls and rough accommodations and no luxuries. Only a few hardy souls were willing to rough it the way the old-time cowboys had.

There were six people in the party, three couples. Four of that number were good riders already, and they weren't afraid of snakes or coyotes or rolling into the camp fire in their sleep. It was a beautiful day, with the ragged mountains ringing around the flat grassy plain, and Nell felt on top of the world as she rode along at the head of the group with Tyler at her side. She kept looking back to make sure she wasn't losing any of their small parade.

"They're doing fine," Tyler told her as he lit a cigarette with steady hands. "Don't worry so much."

"Two of them have never even seen a real horse before," she reminded him.

"The Callaways?" He grinned, referring to a newly married, middle-aged couple who were, to put it politely, well fed. "No, but you've taught them how to stay on, at least, and they're getting the hang of it. Just relax."

She tried, but being a mother hen had become a habit, and she had a bad feeling about doing this camp out without Chappy and the chuck wagon that usually came along with a bigger crowd.

And sure enough, things did begin to go wrong suddenly. They rode for an hour and then turned back toward the ranch house and stopped about a mile out to make camp just before dark.

Mrs. Callaway, a pleasant cheerful little blond lady, came down off her horse too suddenly and caught her blouse on the pommel. There she hung, two inches above the desert floor, while the horse shook his head and pranced restlessly.

Tyler leaped forward to lift Mrs. Callaway while Nell soothed the horse and extricated the blouse.

"Are you all right, Mrs. Callaway?" Nell asked anxiously when the red-faced little woman had stopped shaking in her concerned husband's arms.

"Oh, I'm fine," she said with a grin. "What a story to tell the folks back home!"

Nell relaxed, but Mrs. Callaway's experience was only the beginning. Her husband went to help Tyler and the other men gather brush to make a fire and unearthed a long, fat, very unsocial rattlesnake.

He let out a war whoop, which startled Mrs. Donnegan, who backed into a cactus and let out a war whoop of her own. By the time the rattlesnake was disposed of by Tyler, and Mrs. Donnegan had her cactus spines removed by Nell, everybody was ready to eat. Tyler had a roaring fire going and had passed out wieners and buns and marshmallows and sticks for the guests while he brewed up a pot of black coffee.

"I really hate coffee," Mrs. Harris remarked. She was the only sour note in the bunch, a city woman who'd come to the desert only because her husband had coaxed her into it. She hated the desert, the cactus, the heat, the isolation—she hated everything, in fact. "I'd rather have a soft drink."

"No problem," her husband said. "We'll ride down to the ranch and get one."

"On that horse?" Mrs. Harris wailed, her black eyes going even blacker. "I hurt in places I didn't even know I had!"

"Then you can drink coffee, can't you, sweetheart?" her husband continued.

She pouted, but she shut up. The Callaways sat close together, sharing condiments for the hot dogs while they

munched on potato chips and carried on a casual conversation with the other guests on a variety of newsy
subjects.

Nell enjoyed the quiet wonder of night on the desert as
she never had, especially when Tyler started telling their
guests about the surrounding territory and something of
its history. She hadn't realized how much he knew about
southeastern Arizona, and some of it she hadn't even
known herself.

He talked about places like Cochise Stronghold, where
the famous Apache chief was buried. There was a marker
there, he added, telling that Indian Agent Tom Jeffords,
a friend of Cochise, was the only white man privileged to
know the exact spot of the chief's burial. The Apaches
had run their horses over the ground and dragged it with
brush behind them to conceal forever the place where
Cochise rested.

There was also the famous Copper Queen Hotel in
Bisbee, a landmark from old copper mining days in the
Lavender Pit, where guests drank French champagne and
were entertained by famous singers.

Farther south was Douglas, where Agua Prieta lay just
over the border in Mexico. Pancho Villa had raided the
border town, and a hotel in Douglas bore the marks of
his horse on its marble staircase, which could still be seen
today.

"You know a lot about this part of the state, Mr. Jacobs," Mr. Callaway remarked. "Do you come from
around here?"

"No. I'm from south Texas." He smiled. "Near Vic-
toria. My people founded a little place called Jacobsville, where I was raised."

"I love Texas," Mrs. Callaway said, sighing. "I guess
you have cactus and mesquite and sagebrush..."

"Actually, it's more like magnolias, live oaks and dogwood trees," Tyler mused. "West Texas has those plants you're thinking about."

She blushed. "Sorry."

He laughed out loud. "Don't feel bad, a lot of people don't realize just how many different geographic sections there are in Texas. We've got everything from beach to desert to mountain country and plains. Texas had the option of becoming five separate states if it wanted to. But nobody ever did."

"I can see why," Mrs. Callaway said. "I've heard that you can drive from sunup to sunset and never leave Texas."

"That's very nearly true," he agreed.

"I suppose you'll go back there one day?" the small woman asked.

Tyler looked at Nell, his eyes narrow, thoughtful as they caressed hers until she caught her breath. "Maybe. Maybe not," he added softly, and smiled at Nell.

She felt lighter than air all over again, invincible. She laughed delightedly. "Anybody want more marshmallows?"

They roasted marshmallows until nobody could stuff another one into his mouth, and then they laid out the bedrolls and settled down for the night, while the orange flames of the camp fire drifted lazily back and forth in the faint wind. It was cold on the desert at night. The guests had been told that and were prepared.

Nell moved her sleeping bag close to Tyler's, to his secret delight, and with a shy glance at him as he rested with his saddle for a pillow, she settled down beside him.

"Comfortable?" he asked, his voice deep and soft in the firelit darkness as he turned on his side to watch her.

"Yes." She gave in to the need to look at him, to memorize the lines and curves of his face, his body. She felt a kind of possessiveness toward him that she didn't really understand. "Do you miss Texas, Tyler?" she asked hesitantly.

"I got pretty homesick at first," he conceded. "But there's something about this desert that gets into your blood. It's full of history, but the cities are forward-looking, as well, and there are plenty of conservationists around who care about the land and water resources. Yes, I miss Texas. But I could live here, Nell," he said, smiling at her.

She wanted so badly to ask him if it was just because he liked the land, but she couldn't get the words to form properly. She blurted out, "With Margie?"

His eyebrows lifted. "Did I say with Margie?"

"No, but..."

He reached out a lean hand and touched her fingers where they lay cold and trembling on her stomach. His covered them, warmed them and made her tingle from head to toe. "I told you, Nell, you're going to have to figure it out for yourself. I won't tell you how I feel about Margie, or how I feel about you, for that matter."

"Why?" she asked more plaintively than she knew.

"Because I want you to understand a little more about trust than you do, honey," he replied. "There's a part of you that draws back and shies away from me. Until you get it worked out, I'm not going to influence you one way or the other."

She sighed. "I guess maybe I'll work it out, then."

"Want to come closer?" he coaxed with a warm smile. "You're pretty safe, considering how we're surrounded by curious eyes."

She yielded to the temptation to be close. Inching her way, she moved her sleeping bag right up against his and turned on her side to rest beside him, with her head pillowed on one of his hard arms.

"That's better," he said softly. He eased forward a fraction of an inch and brushed her warm lips gently with his, savoring their faint trembling, their helpless response. "You might keep something in mind," he whispered.

"Oh? What?" she breathed against his lips, and her eyes opened straight into his.

"You aren't wearing makeup or a fancy dress," he whispered quietly. "And I'm not drawing back because you don't appeal to me the way you are."

Her fingers touched his face, loving its strength. "I'm not pretty," she said.

"You are to me," he said. "That's all that matters in the long run, if you'd open your eyes and see what's right under your nose."

"I see you," she said, her voice achingly tender as she adored him with her eyes.

"That's what I mean," he replied. He drew her closer. The saddle protected their faces from prying eyes, and he bent slowly to press his mouth hard against hers. "I want you, Nell," he said into her parted lips as he bit at them.

She wanted him, too. Her body was already on fire, and all he was doing was kissing her. She nibbled helplessly at his teasing mouth, and her hand smoothed into his thick hair, trying to draw him down.

"No," he breathed. "You can't have my mouth that way, not tonight. I can't lose my head with you, honey. There are too many witnesses."

"What if we were alone?" she moaned under her breath. She slid her arms around his neck to press her breasts against his hard chest.

"Nell...damn it." He shuddered. He lifted his tormented eyes to the camp fire. It was dying down and he needed to get up and put some fresh wood on it. The other campers were in their sleeping bags and turned toward the fire in a semicircle, which he and Nell were behind. No one could see them. He realized that now, and his powerful body trembled with the need to ease Nell onto her back and slide his leg between both of hers and show her how much he wanted her. He could feel her skin against his, the silken warmth of her breasts hard tipped under his broad chest, the cries that he could tease out of her throat while he seduced her body slowly and tenderly and penetrated its virginal purity....

He groaned. His fingers on her arms hurt, but she didn't mind. Something powerful and mysterious was working in him, and she was too hungry to be afraid of it. This was Tyler, and she loved him with all her heart. She wanted memories, all that she could get, to press to her mind in the years that would follow.

"What is it?" she asked.

He looked down at her. In the dim light he could see her soft eyes, he could feel her quickened breathing. His hand moved with quiet possession over her blouse and smoothed around her breast until he found the hard tip. He watched her bite her lip and jerk toward him, trying not to cry out lest someone heard her.

"This is not sane," he whispered as the arm under her nape contracted with desire. "Of all the stupid places to make love...."

"Touch me," she whispered brokenly.

His breath was audible as the words shattered his control and made him vulnerable. "Oh, Nell, you can't imagine what I'm thinking." He laughed huskily as his hand slid to the buttons of her blouse and began to lazily unfasten them. "You can't imagine what I want to do to you."

"Yes, I can," she whispered back, "because you told me, remember?" Her eyes met his searchingly. "You told me every single detail."

His powerful body trembled as he reached the last button. "Yes. And I dreamed it that night. Dreamed that I took you under me and felt your body like a field of flowers absorbing me so tenderly." He was whispering, but the tone of his voice drugged her. His fingers slid under the fabric and stopped with delighted surprise when he found nothing except soft warm skin.

Her lips parted. "I've never done this before," she whispered unsteadily. "Gone without . . . without what I usually wear, I mean."

He could have jumped over the moon. His fingers delved farther under the soft fabric and found a hard tip that brought a pleasured gasp from her lips when he touched it. "Lie still, honey," he whispered, his voice as unsteady as her own as he peeled away the cotton. "And for God's sake, don't cry out when I put my mouth on you. . . ."

She had to bite her lower lip almost until it bled to manage that, because his lips were hungry and demanding. When he took her inside the warm darkness of his mouth, she felt tears well up from her closed eyes because it was like a tiny fulfillment in itself. She writhed helplessly, her nails biting him, her mouth as hungry as his, while the stars boiled down around them in white-hot flame.

He drew back first, and suddenly fastened her blouse with trembling hands before he rolled away from her and got to his feet.

She lay there, on fire for him, her eyes watching him as he moved near the camp fire. Her body trembled with a need she'd never felt before. She wanted him, she wanted him!

His back was arrow straight as he began to build up the fire. He stood there for a while, and by the time he came back to his bedroll, her heart was beating normally again and she could feel the tension easing out of her body. But when he climbed into his sleeping bag, the tension came back all over again.

"Tyler," she whispered achingly.

"It passes," he whispered back. "I'm sorry, little one. I didn't mean to take you that far. It's impossible, in more ways than one."

She felt for his lean hand and curled her fingers into it trustingly. "I know. But it was sweet, all the same. I love it when you touch me like that. I'm not even embarrassed to tell you so."

His fingers contracted. "Then I don't mind telling you that I almost couldn't pull back." His head turned and his eyes searched hers in the blazing orange reflection of the fire beyond them. "One day I won't be able to stop. What then?"

Her lips parted. "I don't know."

"You'd better start thinking about it," he said bluntly. "Because things are getting totally out of hand. Either we part company or risk the consequences."

She lowered her worried eyes to the steady rise and fall of his chest. "I...don't want to lose you," she said, burying her pride.

He brought her hand to his mouth. "That would be harder than you realize. Do you still want me, or is it easing off?"

She flushed. "It's easing off," she whispered back.

"At least now you understand why I get short-tempered from time to time, don't you?" he mused.

"Yes." She nuzzled her face against his arm. "What are we going to do?"

"What are *you* going to do?" he said, rephrasing the question. "The ball's in your court, honey. Make your move."

"But what do you want?"

"You."

"Just my body?" she asked softly.

"All of you."

She took a slow breath. "For how long?" she asked bravely.

"I told you, Nell. Love doesn't come with a money-back guarantee—if you do love me. What you feel might be infatuation, or just your first sensual experience making you vulnerable to me."

She searched his face, trying to see if he really believed that. "Is that what you think?"

"Not really. Why don't you tell me what you feel?"

She hesitated, and despite what she did feel, she couldn't lower her pride enough to tell him. She moved her fingers closer into his, feeling his own part and accept them in a warm, strong clasp.

"That reserve is the biggest part of our problem," he murmured. "You won't give in because you don't think I want you."

"I know you want me," she corrected.

"But not how badly, or in what way," he returned. "You're still locked up in the past, afraid of being hurt again."

"I know you wouldn't hurt me," she said unexpectedly, and her eyes were eloquent. "I never knew that a man could be so gentle."

He brought her fingers to his mouth. "That seems to come naturally with you," he said softly. "I've never felt as tender with a woman until now."

She moved her head on his arm. "Tyler, is it just physical with you?"

"If it was," he replied with a dry smile, "would I give a damn about your old-fashioned ideas on chastity? Would I even try to pull back?"

She felt her cheeks burn, and then she laughed self-consciously. "No. Of course not."

"Take it from there and think about it. Now we'd better get some sleep. We've already talked and...other things...for more than an hour."

"It didn't seem that long," she said shyly.

"For me, either, Nell." He let their clasped hands relax between them and closed his eyes. "After tonight," he murmured drowsily, "you'll never be able to deny that we've slept together."

"No, I won't." She curled a little closer and closed her own eyes. Her last thought before she fell asleep was that she'd never felt more secure or happy in all of her life.

She woke at dawn to the delicious smell of percolating coffee and bacon and eggs being fried. Tyler was already hard at work on breakfast, with a little good-intentioned help from a couple of the guests. Everyone ate quietly, enjoying the silence of the desert at dawn and the incredible colors of the sky on the horizon.

"I've never seen anything so beautiful," Mrs. Callaway said with a sigh, nestling close to her husband.

"A living art gallery," Tyler agreed, smiling at Nell. "With a new canvas every minute of the day. It certainly is beautiful." *Like you,* his eyes were telling Nell, wooing her.

She sighed, her heart in her eyes, in her smile, in her rapt attention. His gaze locked with hers while he smoked his cigarette, and the exchange lasted long enough to make her blood run wildly through her veins and her knees get weak.

They rode back to the ranch a few minutes later, and Nell helped Tyler get the horses unsaddled, unbridled and put back in their stalls.

"I've never enjoyed anything more," Nell told him honestly, and laughed uninhibitedly. "It was wonderful."

"I thought so myself," he murmured. He leaned against a closed stall, and his green eyes glittered over her. "Come here," he challenged from deep in his throat.

Her heart raced. She didn't hesitate. She went straight to him and deliberately let her hips melt into his, her legs rest against the powerful strength of his own.

She raised her face for his kiss, blatantly inviting, without fear or inhibitions or reservations.

"Now I want an answer," he said solemnly. "I want to know what you feel for me. I want to know where I stand. You're going to have to trust me enough to tell me."

"That isn't quite fair," she argued. "I have to lower my pride, and you won't lower yours."

"I'm not the one with all the hang-ups," he reminded her. "Any good relationship has to be built on absolute trust to be successful."

"Yes, I know. But . . ." She avoided his gaze.

He tilted her face up to his. "Take a chance, Nell."

She took a deep breath, gathered her courage and started to speak. And just as she opened her mouth, a familiar voice called, "Tyler, darling, there you are! The boys and I arrived yesterday evening, and we're going to spend the week—isn't that nice?"

Nell moved away from Tyler as Margie came laughing into the stable and threw her arms around him. "Oh, you darling man, how have I managed to live all these years without you? Nell, isn't he wonderful? I'm so happy! Tyler, have you told her our news?" she prompted, her face radiant.

"No, he hasn't," Nell said, turning away. "But he doesn't need to, now. I can guess. See you later. I need a bath and a change of clothing."

"Nell," Tyler called after her, but she wasn't listening. She kept going into the house, with her dreams around her ears. Only a blind fool wouldn't know what Margie had hinted at. She and Tyler had something going, it was just plain obvious. And how could he have touched Nell so hungrily only last night, knowing that Margie was going to be here, waiting for him? Nell could have thrown things. Once again she'd been taken in by her own stupid, trusting nature. Well, this was the last straw. She was going to call Uncle Ted and tell him he could keep the ranch forever—she was going to leave and find something else to do. And as far away from Arizona and Tyler Jacobs as she could get!

Chapter Ten

"What do you look so unhappy for?" Bella asked Nell. "Didn't you enjoy the camp out?"

"It was all right," Nell said with deliberate carelessness. She didn't want to remember what she and Tyler had done together. Margie had spoiled everything. Whatever Tyler had been going to say would never be said, and it looked as though Margie had pulled out all the stops and was going after him headlong.

"Hand me that mixer." Bella nodded toward the appliance she was going to use on a cake mix. "That Mrs. Norman was back in here again complaining about the menu. She's another Mrs. Harris, but at least Mr. Harris is here. Mrs. Norman doesn't like the way I cook. And besides all that, she thinks the entertainment stinks and there's nothing to do but ride horses."

Nell's eyes bulged. "Did you tell her that this is a dude ranch? People come here to ride horses."

"I told her that and plenty more." Bella looked at the younger woman sheepishly. "She's packing to leave. She says she's going to tell the whole world what a miserable operation we've got here. Oh, and we don't even have a tennis pro," she added.

"Tyler fired him, along with the golf pro," Nell reminded her. "He said they weren't paying their way."

"You mad at me?" Bella asked.

Nell put her arms around the older woman. "I love you. If people say cruel things about your cooking, they deserve to be sent packing. I think you're terrific."

Bella smiled and hugged her back. "That goes double for me. But I'll apologize all the same, if you want me to."

"No. Mrs. Norman may leave, with my blessing. In fact," she said, moving toward the door, "I'll even refund her money."

"Tyler won't like that," Bella called after her.

"Tyler can eat worms and die," Nell muttered.

"So that's it," Bella said to herself, and giggled once Nell was out of earshot.

Mrs. Norman had finished packing. She had her full-length mink coat wrapped around her thin body and her black eyes were flashing. "I am leaving," she told Nell, who was waiting outside the apartment when the older woman came out with her nose haughtily in the air. "You may have someone bring my luggage and call me a cab."

"With pleasure," Nell said, and even smiled. "If you'll stop by the office, I'll gladly refund your money."

Mrs. Norman eyed her suspiciously. "Why?"

"You don't like it here," Nell said. "There's no reason you should pay to be made miserable. The cooking is terrible, there's nothing to do..."

Mrs. Norman actually squirmed and pulled the mink coat closer, despite the fact that it was ninety degrees outside and she was already sweating. "That won't be necessary," she said. "Money is the least of my problems." She averted her eyes, then suddenly blurted out, "I'm allergic to horses and the dust is choking me. All my husband's friends go to dude ranches, and he sent me here because he didn't want to take me to Europe with him." She lifted her chin proudly, even though it trembled. "It's just that…that this room…is so empty," she finished, choking the words out. "I'm so alone."

She broke down into tears and Nell did what came naturally. She took the weeping woman in her arms and just stood holding her and rocking her and murmuring soft words of reassurance.

"There's nothing wrong with the food," Mrs. Norman said with a hiccup. Mascara ran like black tears from her huge, hurting eyes. "It's delicious. And the people are nice, too, but they're all couples. My husband only married me as a business proposition—he doesn't even like me. He never tried to make our marriage anything else."

"You might consider that men don't read minds," Nell told her gently, and even as she said it she smiled inwardly at the irony of telling this sophisticated woman anything about men, when her own love life was so confusing and unfamiliar. "Your husband might think you didn't want to go with him."

Mrs. Norman pulled away self-consciously and dried her eyes with a pure white linen handkerchief. Then she smiled a little shakily. "I'm sorry, I never go to pieces like this." She blew her nose. "Actually, he asked me if I wanted to go, and I laughed at him. He's not a handsome man, but I . . . I do love him." She glanced at Nell. "Can I make a long-distance call to Europe and have it charged to my account?"

"Of course you can!" Nell smiled. "He might even decide to come back home."

Mrs. Norman smiled back, suddenly looking ten years younger. "I'll do it right now." She took off the mink coat. "That's my security blanket," she added ruefully, draping it over one arm. "I hate the damned thing, it makes me sneeze, and it's too hot to wear it anywhere except during blizzards in Alaska. I'll just make that phone call." She went inside the apartment, and before she closed the door she turned to look at Nell. "Thank you," she said sincerely.

Nell couldn't get over what had just happened. She felt on top of the world; she'd just learned a valuable lesson about human nature, and she might have helped save a marriage.

It wasn't a good time for Tyler to come around the corner of the apartment block, glaring into space.

He stopped, looking at her. "Are you lost?" he asked.

"Not lately." She put her hands in her back pockets and studied him quietly. "You look peaked."

"Do I? Why did you go rushing out of the stable?" he demanded.

She lifted her eyebrows. "Three is still a crowd, isn't it?"

"You thought I might have been waiting breathlessly for you to leave so that I could seduce Margie in one of the stalls?" he said with a cold tone to his deep voice.

Put that way, it sounded ridiculous. "Well, I guess not. But she was waiting for you."

"She had some good news. You won't get to hear it, of course," he continued. He lit a cigarette and threw her a mocking smile. "Margie and I don't think you deserve to hear it. You jump to conclusions on the shabbiest evidence, and you won't listen to explanations. You're still running away from involvement."

"I've had some hard knocks in the past," she defended herself.

"I know all about that," he said. "I wormed the rest of it out of Margie, and I'm sorry about what happened to you. But I thought you and I were on the way to something more important than a few stolen kisses—yet I still can't get close to you."

She flushed, remembering the trail ride. "I wouldn't exactly say that," she faltered.

"I'm not talking about physical closeness," he said curtly. "I can't get close to you emotionally. You back away from me."

"I have good reason to!" she shot back.

"Not with me, you don't," he said, his voice deep and quiet as he watched her. "I'm not asking you to move in with me, or even to spend the night with me in a nonplatonic way. I want you to trust me, Nell."

"But I do trust you," she began.

"Not in the way that counts." He drew in a slow breath. "Well, I've had all I can take. I won't run after you, honey. If you want anything more to happen between us, you'll have to make the first move. I'm not going to touch you again. You're going to have to decide."

He moved away without another word, leaving Nell to stand there and watch him leave with her heart down around her ankles.

Mrs. Norman left in a delighted flurry that afternoon. Her husband had been thrilled to hear from her, and he'd decided to come home and meet her in Vermont for a second honeymoon. Nell had driven the older woman to the airport and had been fervently hugged before Mrs. Norman ran like a teenage girl to catch her plane.

At least someone was happy, Nell thought miserably. But it sure wasn't her. She still didn't understand why Tyler was trying to make her chase him. It didn't really make sense. He was the man, and the man was supposed to make all the moves, not the woman; at least, not in Nell's old-fashioned world.

Of course, Tyler was old-fashioned, too. That was the hard thing to reconcile. And with his attitude, it didn't really make sense that he'd be hanging around Nell when he wanted Margie. And he had to want Margie. Every man did. Margie was beautiful and cultured and sophisticated, just the right kind of woman for a man like Tyler.

During the next few days, Margie kept very much to herself. She smiled at Nell as if nothing were wrong, but she spent a lot of time where the men—especially Tyler—were, and she kept the boys with her. She seemed to understand that her presence irritated Nell, and she did everything she could to make it bearable for the younger woman, right down to sleeping late and going to bed early.

Nell was actually looking for an excuse for a confrontation, because there was a lot she wanted to say to her sister-in-law. But Margie made that impossible, and even Tyler interfered if it looked as though Nell might find an opportunity. So the days went by with Nell getting more frustrated by the minute. What she didn't know was that

Darren McAnders had been furious that Margie was spending time with Tyler, and had begun to make his presence felt and heard while Tyler and Nell were away on the camp out. He and Margie had it out that very evening while the camp out was in full swing. The argument shortly began to have results. When no one was looking, McAnders picked Margie up and carried her off to a quiet spot under the big palo verde tree near the apartments. And there he kissed her until she couldn't stand up or protest. Then he began to tell her how he felt and what he wanted. When he finished, she was smiling. And the next kiss was instigated by her. But they kept their secret, because Margie didn't want to spring anything on Nell until Tyler had a chance to patch things up with his lady. Margie was getting impatient, though. Tyler and Nell seemed to have reached an impasse.

Nell went on teaching the daily riding lessons and avoided going to the dinner table until she was sure it was too late for Tyler to be there, if he'd decided to eat at the big house, that was. He spent more and more time in the bunkhouse or his own cabin.

Nights got longer and Nell's temper got shorter. Until Tyler had come along, she'd never known that she even had a temper, but he seemed to bring out the beast in her.

It was like being half a person. She strained for glimpses of him; she spun beautiful daydreams about him. Her eyes followed him everywhere. But she kept to herself, and spoke to him only when he asked her something directly. Which was all she could do, because he was still spending time with Margie. Actually he was chaperoning her with McAnders so that Bella wouldn't figure out their secret and spill the beans too soon, but Nell didn't know that and she didn't trust him.

Tyler was brooding, too. He almost gave up. Nell seemed more unapproachable now than she ever had, and she was retreating by the day. He wondered if he was ever going to be able to reach her again.

Texas seemed so far away. He remembered how he'd taken Abby Clark out on a date and how sweet it had been to dance with her. But it was nothing compared to the feel of Nell's body in his arms, her soft, shy mouth under the crush of his, welcoming him. She had a big heart and he wanted it, but Nell didn't seem to want him back.

She thought he was stuck on Margie, and that was a real laugh. Margie reminded him too much of the world he'd had to give up, of all he'd lost. He was going to need a woman who wasn't interested in frills and fancies, a woman who'd be willing to work at his side and help him start over. Nell was just right, in every way, and he cared about her deeply. The problem was getting her to believe he loved her when she had such poor self-image. She couldn't or wouldn't believe that she was infinitely desirable to him. And until he could break her out of that self-ordained mold, he was never going to reach her.

His green eyes glittered as he saw her riding back in from the trail ride with Darren McAnders at her side. Damn McAnders. Why couldn't he stop interfering?

He watched them dismount. McAnders took Nell's mount by the bridle and led both horses into the stable, with a grin and a cheerful greeting to Tyler.

Tyler didn't acknowledge it. He stood glaring at Nell for a long moment, and then he strode toward her.

She watched the way he walked, so tall and easy, which was deceptive. He was all muscle, and she knew the power in that exquisitely male body, the sweetness of being held by him while he brought her every nerve alive. He had on a beige shirt that emphasized his dark coloring, made his green eyes even greener. He came close and she felt the tension grow between them almost instantly.

"Having fun?" he asked.

She didn't like his tone. It was insulting. "No, I'm not," she replied tersely. "I hate running a dude ranch. I'm scared to death that a rattlesnake is going to bite somebody or a horse is going to run away with a greenhorn rider or that we're going to lose somebody out on that desert and find them several days later. I hate budgeting, I don't like the need to cut out half of our recreational facilities, and if I have to hear one more remark about how desolate and disgusting my desert is, I'm going to scream!"

"I just asked if you were having fun," he pointed out. "I didn't ask for a rundown on world economy."

"Don't mind me," she said mockingly. "Pat yourself on the back."

He did, and her face flamed with bad temper.

"Why don't you go back to Texas?" she muttered.

"Oh, I like it here," he told her. "Dust and rattlesnakes grow on a man."

Her eyes narrowed. "Don't you start," she dared.

His eyebrows lifted. "What a nasty temper you're in, little Nell. Why don't you go and eat something bland and see if it'll take the pepper off your tongue?"

"I'm going to tell my uncle how you're ruining the place," she threatened.

"He won't listen," he said with a lazy grin. "He's too busy depositing the money we've been making lately."

She took a sharp breath. "That's it, go ahead, put all the blame on me!"

"Mind you don't split a blood vessel with all that temper, honey," he said.

"Don't call me honey!"

"How about vinegar?"

She aimed a kick at his shin, but he was faster. He caught her up in his arms and carried her toward the corral, where the horses' watering trough was sitting innocently.

Through her kicking and cursing, she noticed where he was headed and clung to his neck.

"You wouldn't dare," she snapped.

He chuckled. "Of course I would."

Her arms tightened. "I'll take you with me."

"Promises, promises," he breathed huskily, and his mouth lowered so that it almost touched hers. "Will you, indeed?"

The threat of his lips made her heart race. She felt her breasts pressed against his chest; she smelled the leather and tobacco scent of his body mingling with the cologne he wore. She felt the strength of the arms under her and a kind of feminine delight in his maleness grew within her.

"Will I what?" she breathed. Her nails scraped gently against his nape as unfamiliar sensations trembled through her.

"Don't tease," he whispered. "If I start kissing you now, we're going to have the biggest audience this side of Denver."

Her lips parted. "I'm not teasing," she said softly.

His face hardened. "No? Then tell me how I feel about Margie."

She felt the spell shatter. "I don't know," she muttered. "Anyway, it's none of my business."

"The hell it isn't. You blind little bat!"

And with a suddenness that put her between shock and fear, his mouth went down on hers savagely for one long instant before he took advantage of her helpless reaction and threw her, bottom first, right into the horses' trough.

Chapter Eleven

Tyler had strode off in a black temper by the time Nell dragged herself, dripping and swearing, out of the horses' trough. A couple of the men were watching, and she gave them her best glare as she sloshed off toward the house. It didn't help her dignity that they were laughing behind her.

She stormed into the house and upstairs to shower and change her clothes before anybody got a good look at her and guffawed some more. Then she returned downstairs, cooler but still fuming, and dialed her Uncle Ted's number with fingers that trembled in her haste. And all the while she wanted to fling Tyler and Margie down a mine shaft.

"Hello?" A deep, masculine voice came over the other end.

"Hello, yourself. I don't want to run this ranch anymore," she said without preamble. "I don't care if it means I lose everything, I won't stay at the same place with that foreman of yours!''

Uncle Ted was getting a new lease on life. His man-hating niece was suddenly losing her temper, something she never did, and over a real live man! He could have jumped for joy. He knew it had been a good idea to send Tyler Jacobs out to the Double R.

''Now, now,'' Uncle Ted soothed, ''I can't let you throw away your inheritance, Nell. No, you'll just have to stay there and work things out, I'm afraid.''

''I can't!'' she wailed. ''Look, I'll sign everything over to you—''

''No.'' He hung up.

She stared at the dead receiver as if it had sprouted flowers. Talk about finality! He hadn't even said good-bye.

She slammed the receiver down with a bang and glared at it. ''I hate you!'' she raged. ''I think you're an over-bearing male chauvinist, and just because you're rich doesn't give you the right to try and run people's lives for them!''

She was screaming by now, and Curt and Jess, stand-ing unnoticed in the doorway, were watching her with saucer-size eyes. They motioned to their mother, who joined the rapt audience.

''I don't want him here,'' she fumed at the telephone. ''I never did! I don't understand why you wouldn't give me a chance to straighten things out by myself before you stuck your big nose into my business. It's my ranch, my father left it to me and Teddy, and he never meant for you to dangle it over my head like a guillotine!''

''What's a guillotine?'' Jess whispered to his mother.

"It's stuff you put on your joints when you have rheumatism," Curt whispered.

"Hush!" said their mother.

"Well, you can just tell him to go back to Texas, or I'll go there and live myself and he can have the ranch! I hate him, and I hate you, and I hate Margie, too!"

"It must be the insecticides in the groundwater table affecting your brain," Margie said, shaking her head.

Nell whirled, aghast to find three pairs of eyes staring at her. She stared back, speechless.

"Aunty Nell, why are you talking to the telephone?" Curt wanted to know.

"I was talking to your Great-Uncle Ted," she said with mangled dignity.

"Wouldn't you communicate better by talking into the receiver?" Margie mused.

Nell glared at her. "I haven't congratulated you yet. I'll make sure I send you a suitable gift when the time comes."

"How sweet of you, Nell." Margie sighed. "He's sooo handsome, and I can't believe he really loves me."

"We love him, too," the boys chorused, grinning. "And we can come and live here now—"

Nell screamed. She actually screamed. She did it and then stood stock-still, astonished that the sound had really come from her throat.

"I love you, too." Margie added fuel to the fire, making a kissing motion with her lips. "We'll be one big happy family."

"Like hell we will!" Nell burst out, and tears fell from her eyes. "I'm leaving, right now!"

"Leaving for where?" Margie asked.

"I don't know and I don't...care." She hiccuped from stuffy tears. "Oh, Margie, how could you!"

"Boys, go and find a new lizard to scare me with," Margie told her sons. She shooed them out and closed the door.

"I want to leave," Nell wailed.

"After you listen to me," Margie said. "Now dry up for a minute. How do you feel about Tyler?"

Nell tried to avoid the question, but Margie wouldn't budge. She drew in a shaky breath. "I . . . love him," she bit off.

Margie smiled. "Do you? A lot?"

"Yes."

"But you think that he's the kind of man who plays with one woman at the same time he's courting somebody else?"

Nell blinked. She turned her head slightly, and her great, dark eyes fixed on Margie's face. "Well, no, actually, he isn't," she admitted. "He's kind of old-fashioned about things."

Margie nodded. "That's right. You're doing very well, darling. Keep going."

"If he'd been going to marry you, he'd have told me himself," Nell ventured. "He wouldn't have let me find out by accident from someone else."

"Yes. And?"

Nell drew in a slow, exquisite breath. "He'd never play around with an innocent woman unless he was serious about her. Unless he was playing for keeps."

Margie smiled gently. "And you were going to cuss out Uncle Ted and run away."

Nell dried her tears. "I've been such a fool. I was scared, you know, Margie."

"We're all scared. Commitment isn't easy, even when people love each other." She went close to Nell, smiling. "I'm going to marry Darren. Will you be my maid of honor?"

Nell burst out laughing. "Oh, Margie, of course I will!" She hugged the older woman fervently, laughing and crying all at once. "I'm so sorry for the things I said. I was so jealous, and my heart was broken! But now I think I'm going to be all right, after all."

"I know you are. Wouldn't you like to take a nice, refreshing walk?" she added. "You might walk down by the holding pens. The scenery there is really something."

"Nice, is it?" Nell probed.

"Dark and handsome, to coin a phrase." Margie grinned. "But it may not last long, so you'd better hurry."

"I'll do that. But first, can you lend me a dress? Something very feminine and lighter than air and suitable for a woman to chase a man in?"

Margie was delighted. "You bet I can. Come on!"

It was a dream of a dress in creamy spring green with a full, flowing skirt and a pretty rounded neckline and puffy sleeves. Nell felt like a young girl again, all heart and nerves as she brushed her long, clean hair and put on makeup and a little perfume.

Nell smiled, thinking how sweet it was going to be to make her first move toward Tyler, to flirt openly with him, sure of herself at last.

She slipped on a pair of soft shoes and tore down the staircase and out the door toward the holding pens. It seemed to take forever to get there, and she was breathless from her haste when she finally reached them.

The pens were empty now, with roundup over, but Tyler was leaning back lazily against the fence with a cigarette in his fingers, his long legs crossed and one arm propped on the second fence rail. His hat was pulled low over his eyes so that Nell couldn't quite see them through the shadows, but he looked approachable enough.

"Hello," she said nervously.

He nodded. His green eyes glittered over her possessively before he turned back to the horizon and took a draw from his cigarette. "Lose your way?"

"Not this time." She went closer and stood beside him to look over the pasture. "Do you make a habit of throwing women into water troughs? Because if you do, we're going to have a rocky life together."

He couldn't believe he'd heard that. He turned, his eyes hungry on her face, his pulse racing. She'd dressed up and fixed her face and hair, and she looked radiant. "No, I don't make a habit of it," he replied. "But at the time I'd had about all I could stand. Nell, I'm thinking of going back to Texas."

"Running out on me?" she asked with pure bravado. "I'll come after you."

He touched his forehead unobtrusively to see if he was dying of fever or having hallucinations. "I beg your pardon?"

She gathered up her shaken nerve. "I said, I'll follow you back to Texas."

He finished the cigarette and ground it out under his boot, taking so long to speak that Nell felt her knees getting ready to buckle in case she'd gotten it wrong and he didn't care.

"No doubts?" he asked suddenly, and his eyes met hers with a fiercely sensual impact.

It was hard to get enough breath to answer him, because he was even closer now, and she had to fight not to put her body right against his and hold on for dear life. "No doubts, Ty," she whispered. She looked up at him and went for broke. "I love you."

His eyes closed for an instant and then opened on a heavy exhaled breath. "My God." He drew her into his arms and held her there, rocking her hungrily from side to side, with his lips on her cheek, her ear, her neck, and finally, crushing into the warmth of her soft mouth.

She held on to him with all her strength, loving the furious beating of her heart, the weakness he engendered in her body, the warm wonder of knowing that he cared about her, too. She sighed under his devouring mouth and it lifted, fractionally, while he searched her eyes with all the barriers gone.

"Did Margie tell you that it isn't me she's going to marry?" he asked quietly.

"Not really," she hedged, because it was a dangerous time to go into all the details.

He frowned. "She didn't talk to you?"

"It was more a case of her making *me* talk. And I worked it out by myself." She smiled tenderly at him. "If you were going to marry Margie," she began quietly, "you'd never have touched me, not even out of pity."

He didn't move for a minute. Then he began to stroke her bare arms very gently with his warm, work-roughened hands. "It took you a long time to realize that," he said deeply, and his heart sang because of the look in her eyes.

"Yes," she said with a faint grin. "Of course, I didn't work it out at first. After I got out of the horses' trough and dried off," she said with a glare that didn't faze him, "I called Uncle Ted and yelled at him and told him what he could do with the ranch and that I was leaving forever. He just hung up on me. I guess I'll have to call him back and apologize.''

"I wouldn't just yet," Tyler advised. "He's probably laughing too hard. I get the idea that before I came along, you never yelled at anybody."

She nodded. "There was never any reason to." She sighed, looking hungrily at his dark face. "Oh, I want you," she whispered, letting down her pride. "I want to live with you and have children with you and grow old with you."

"And what do I want, do you think?" he asked, leading her on.

It didn't work. She just smiled. "You want me, of course."

He burst out laughing, the sound full with joy and delight. He lifted her up against his chest to kiss her with exquisite tenderness. "I'm sorry about the horses' trough. I'd waited and hoped, and we were almost there, and then Margie came along after the camp out and set us back several weeks. She didn't mean to. Her news, of course, was that she and McAnders were engaged. But when you took off, she decided to keep the secret a while longer."

"I'm sorry about that," she murmured. "I didn't think I could compete with her. I never dreamed that you could feel for me what I felt for you. It was like wishing for the moon."

"Not anymore, is it?" he mused, and brushed his mouth sensually across hers.

"Not anymore," she agreed huskily.

"When were you sure that I didn't want Margie?"

"When I remembered that you'd made the sweetest kind of love to me, without asking me to go all the way with you," she whispered, and for the first time, she kissed him, with shy hunger. "And a man like you wouldn't do that unless he had something permanent in mind. Because I'm still a virgin," she breathed into his mouth. "And you're an old-fashioned man. You even said so."

"It took you long enough to remember it," he murmured dryly. He nuzzled her cheek with his, floating, warm from the touch of her body against his, the clasp of her soft arms. "I love you, Nell," he whispered huskily. "And I do want you for keeps. You and a houseful of children and the best future we can make together."

"I love you, too," she whispered fervently.

"You grew on me," he mused, lifting his head to search her soft eyes. "But long before that time I was sick and you nursed me, I knew I'd lost my heart. I wasn't able to think about another woman after that."

"I'm very glad. I loved you from the beginning, although I was afraid to. You see, I thought you were just being nice to me because you felt sorry for me."

"I liked you," he said simply. "And when you started avoiding me, it was like a knife in my heart."

"I didn't think you could care about someone like me," she said quietly. "Then after you began to talk about my low self-image and my lack of confidence, I started thinking about things. I guess none of us is perfect, but that doesn't mean we can't be loved. It doesn't have much to do with beauty and sophistication and money, does it? Love is more than that."

"Much more." He framed her face and bent slowly to her mouth. "I'll cherish you all my life. I don't have a lot to give you, but you can have my heart."

She smiled against his mouth. "I'd rather have that than anything else in the whole world. I'll give you mine for it."

He smiled back. "That," he whispered before he kissed her, "is a deal."

A long time later, they walked back to the house hand in hand, and Margie and the boys and Bella stood on the porch, anxious to find out what had happened.

"Well?" Bella demanded, out of patience. "Is it going to be a wedding or a farewell party?"

"A wedding." Nell laughed and ran forward to hug Bella and Margie and the boys. "And we're going to be so happy together."

"As if anybody could believe otherwise," Bella said, sniffing. "Well, I'll go cook supper. Something special." Her eyes narrowed in thought. "And a cake...."

"You snake in the grass, leading me on like that!" Nell accused Margie. "Making me so jealous that I couldn't stand it!"

"I knew it would either open your eyes or close them for good." Margie smiled. "You could have gone on forever the way you were, untrusting and alone. I thought you needed a chance."

"Well, thank you," Nell said. She glanced at Tyler's radiant expression and then back at Margie as the other woman started to speak.

"I love Darren so much, Nell. Are you going to mind having us both on the place? Because he insists that he's going to support me."

"I don't have any problem at all with that," Nell said at once.

"I called Uncle Ted back after you went out to meet Tyler," Margie said with a secretive smile. "He said if you and Tyler got married, he'd turn over control of the ranch early—as a wedding present."

Tyler didn't say anything, and Nell went close to him. "Look," she said, "it isn't much of a ranch right now. It's lost a lot of money and times are still pretty bad. You are getting nothing but a headache, so don't look on it as a handout."

That took the bitter look off his face. "Then I guess you and I are going to have the challenge of building it up again," he said finally, and his hard features relaxed. He had to start back somewhere, and he loved Nell. The two of them together, working to build a future and a family. Yes, that sounded good. He smiled down at her. "Okay, honey. We'll give it a try."

"And Darren and I can live in the cabin with the boys," Margie suggested. "Or we can build a house close by. I think I'd rather do that. I still have a nest egg, and so does Darren—he's been saving for years. We'll do that. Your foreman will have to have someplace to live."

Tyler glanced amusedly at Nell. "I thought we might offer it to Chappy. He's been here a long time, and he bosses everybody around anyway. What do you think?"

Nell laughed. "I think it's a great idea!"

"So do I," Margie agreed. "Well, shall we go inside and call Uncle Ted one more time?"

Nell slid her hand into Tyler's, and they followed the others back inside. Tyler looked down at her just before they went through the open door. The look on his face made Nell catch her breath. The awe and wonder of love blazed from it as surely as the Arizona sun warmed the desert. Nell's own face reflected a love for her long, tall Texan that would last forever.

*   *   *   *   *

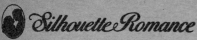

Silhouette Romance

A Trilogy by Diana Palmer

Bestselling Diana Palmer has rustled up three rugged heroes in a trilogy sure to lasso your heart! The titles of the books are your introduction to these unforgettable men:

CALHOUN

In June, you met Calhoun Ballenger. He wanted to protect Abby Clark from the world, but could he protect her from himself?

JUSTIN

In August, Calhoun's brother, Justin—the strong, silent type—had a second chance with the woman of his dreams, Shelby Jacobs.

TYLER

October's long, tall Texan is Shelby's virile brother, Tyler, who teaches shy Nell Regan to trust her instincts—especially when they lead her into his arms!

Don't miss TYLER, the last of three gripping stories from Silhouette Romance!

TALES OF THE RISING MOON
A Desire trilogy by Joyce Thies

MOON OF THE RAVEN—June (#432)
Conlan Fox was part American Indian and as tough as the Montana land he rode, but it took fragile yet strong-willed Kerry Armstrong to make his dreams come true.

REACH FOR THE MOON—August (#444)
It would take a heart of stone for Steven Armstrong to evict the woman and children living on his land. But when Steven saw Samantha, eviction was the last thing on his mind!

GYPSY MOON—October (#456)
Robert Armstrong met Serena when he returned to his ancestral estate in Connecticut. Their fiery temperaments clashed from the start, but despite himself, Rob was falling under the Gypsy's spell.

COMING NEXT MONTH

#610 ITALIAN KNIGHTS— Sharon De Vita
Sal had been Annie's protector since she was widowed, so why hadn't he noticed how beautiful she was? She wouldn't be a widow for long—or his name wasn't Smooth, Suave Sal....

#611 A WOMAN OF SPIRIT—Lucy Gordon
Parapsychologist Dr. Damaris Sherwood thought a Victorian castle was ideal for finding a fascinating phantom. Instead, she found Boyd Radnor—ruggedly real and a man to make her spirits soar!

#612 NOVEMBER RETURNS—Octavia Street
Spunky political consultant Maggie McGraw and handsome lawyer Peter Barnes supported opposing candidates in the election, but Peter was campaigning to show her that they could win love's race—together.

#613 FIVE-ALARM AFFAIR—Marie Ferrarella
Dashing fireman Wayne Montgomery had conquered the inferno in widow Aimee Greer's kitchen, but could she take a chance and let him light a fire in her heart?

#614 THE DISCERNING HEART—Arlene James
Private maid Cheyenne Cates was hired to spy on reclusive Tyler Crawford. She never expected they would fall in love, but would she lose him when he discovered her deceit?

#615 GUARDIAN ANGEL—Nicole Monet
Self-defense instructor Alicia Mason had reluctantly agreed to marry devilish, macho Clint Kelly out of family obligation. But now her heart needed defending against his heavenly charms....

AVAILABLE THIS MONTH:

In October
Silhouette Special Edition
becomes
more special than ever
as it premieres
its sophisticated new cover!

Look for six soul-satisfying novels
every month . . . from
Silhouette Special Edition